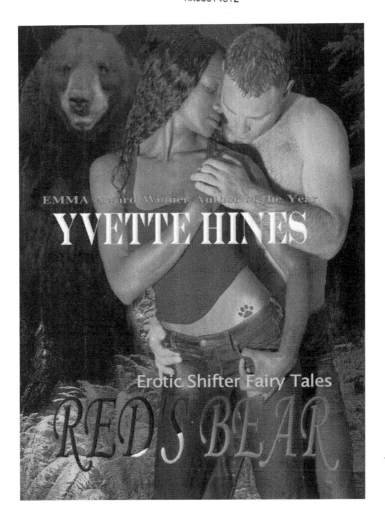

EMMA Award Winner Author of the Year

YVETTE HINES

Erotic Shifter Fairy Tales

RED'S BEAR

Red's Bear

Erotic Shifter Fairy Tales

Yvette Hines

Red's Bear
Copyright © 2013, Yvette Hines
Cover Artist: Antwan Williams
Editor: Bernadette Schane

DEDICATION

To my husband. I love you and I'm so happy that every year brings us closer together as we grow and change. We can overcome all challenges set before us. Thanks to all my author friends on FB, when I hit the dark moment with this book and 'lost it', I think you all for your encouragement and tips. Most of all for understanding my agony and just being there. For my editor, B, I had a hell of a stressful two weeks with this book, then you jumped in and helped things make sense. Thank you so much. To the readers that loved *Bear's Gold* and asked for the next erotic fairy tale in Den County, this is for you.

PROLOGUE

"Ah! This is so frustrating. I'm never going to get it." She jerked the fishing pole out of the water and stared down at her empty line, the bait now missing.

"Yes, you will. It just takes a little patience." Reaching over, he grabbed the hook from her, making sure he didn't pierce her fingers with it.

"What it takes is being smarter than the average fish." She pushed her bottom lip out in a mock pout.

His gaze zoned in on that full bottom lip. All day he'd been tempted by her mouth and more than once he'd wondered what it would be like to kiss her.

She licked her lips and the corners of her mouth trembled in nervousness. The small movement broke his focus.

He didn't want to make her uncomfortable. Glancing away, he pulled a worm out of the bucket at his side, using that small moment to get himself under control. Other teens, his friends, were splashing around in the water fifty or so yards downstream from where he sat on the pier beside her.

"Not really," he replied.

"It's a good thing I don't eat fish, because I would starve."

Looking at her, he frowned. He'd never heard of anyone that didn't eat fish. "Really? You don't eat it?"

"I'm allergic."

He became concerned. "Is it going to bother you to touch it once you've caught one?"

She laughed. "I'll have to catch one first."

Smiling, he nodded. "True."

"No worries. I won't start breaking out in hives or anything from contact."

That made him more at ease. The thought of her being hurt pulled at his core. The urge to protect her was like a stone in his gut: heavy and unable to be ignored. "Okay. Let me show you how to put the worm on the hook more secure so the fish have to work harder to get it. This usually causes them to get stuck on the line."

She scooted her hip toward his, moving closer as she stared at his hands.

Heat raced through his body that had nothing to do with the summer sun beating down on the lake and them. As a sixteen-year-old male who had more than a few encounters with females, he couldn't understand his response to the teen girl beside him. Just on the cusp of womanhood, she was more awkward and graceless than any other girl he knew. Most of the females his age were strong, swift and lithe.

So, why does she affect me?

"Watch how I do this." Spearing the worm with the point of the hook, he threaded it tightly until none of the body was dangling. "Now you try it."

Reaching around him, she bravely took a slimy worm from the tub, it wiggled and twisted around her finger. As she shifted back, her arm brushed his back.

Fire licked up his spine at the brief contact.

Swallowing, he calmed himself the best he could. Speaking around the tightness in his throat, he instructed her on the technique.

"Perfect. Now cast it into the water again."

Once that was complete, they both watched the hooked bait sink below the surface of the lake.

He wanted to talk to her about something. Anything. However his mind had gone blank.

She appeared to be content just setting there in the sun, so he didn't push a conversation.

Feet dangling over the side, they sat and waited.

"Oh, goodness. I have a bite!" She screamed and almost dropped her pole in excitement.

Reaching out, he grabbed the pole above her hands. "I'll help you hold it while you reel it in."

Soon she had the large fish pulled in, taken off the hook and tossed into the wicker basket his grandmother had made him.

"I did it! I did it!" Seated, she bounced up and down on the wooden slats and cheered. "Thank you so much."

Before he knew what to expect, she wrapped her arms around his shoulders in a hug. Stunned for only a moment, he slipped his arms around her waist.

"Yes, you did." It took all of his strength not to glide his hands up and down her back, but he managed to keep them still. "You'll be a pro before the summer is over."

"You think so?" She leaned back, but not enough to break their hold as she gazed into his eyes.

Her eyes were hazel, green with golden-brown flecks in them. He knew it had to do with her heredity.

Staring into her eyes, his core tightened. Like a fish on a string, he was drawn to her. Unable to fight it any longer, he gave in to desire. Setting his lips on hers, he claimed her.

If the sky had opened up and lightning had struck him, he wouldn't have been more shocked by the fiery current that went through him. A combination of lust and protection swirled through his core.

Mine.

This female was his. He and his bear agreed.

The world around them exploded. A woman's angry tones called out to the girl as she came running down the path from the house in a rage.

With her face flushed from the sun and embarrassment, the girl shoved away from him and rushed to meet her mother.

He tried to make sense of everything that had happened as he watched the girl being dragged away.

The sound of splashing water clued him in to the fact the other teens had come closer.

"What's going on, man?" his best friend asked.

Once the girl was out of sight in the house, he faced the group in the water. "I'm not completely sure myself."

"Wow…amazing…"

Frowning at the brown-haired girl in the water, he asked, "What's so amazing about any of this?"

His cousin, a blonde male teen, splashed water up at him. "Your eyes have gone gold."

CHAPTER ONE

"I can't eat. I'm still nauseous all the time and the medicine you gave me has seemed to make matters worse. Over the last two months I've called out two to three times a week from work. Already once this week and it's only Monday."

"Rena, sometimes things like this take time to discover what is going on." Dr. Jung-tu, a small-framed Asian woman with almond-shaped brown eyes, reached out and patted her knee, giving Rena a sympathetic smile.

But, Rena Hoodman didn't want sympathy, she wanted results. Solutions. "How much time? I've been like this for months." Rena hated the whine in her voice, but the aching in her belly was getting progressively worse.

"I've already run a battery of tests with new results. It is not the flu, food poisoning or an intestinal virus." When Rena opened her mouth to speak, the doctor raised her hand to stop her. "I am not giving up and I will run more tests. For now, stop the anti-nausea medication and see if that was just prolonging it." She looked at the computer screen and tapped notes into Rena's medical record.

Sighing, Rena shook her head and pulled the paper gown tighter around her body. She was cold. Odd, because she was rarely cold. She was even happy to give up the meds, she hated taking them, but she'd hoped today she'd have a few more answers.

"Keep the BRAT diet going. Bananas, rice, apple sauce and toast. Remember bland is best."

"I'm trying, Dr. Jung-tu. I really am. But there's a problem."

Her doctor lifted her right eyebrow.

Gazing down at her fingers watching them twist the fragile paper dress, Rena said, "While you're running tests can you please check my iron. It has to be low. I've had cravings for fish. Seafood and honey." She glanced back up.

Astonished, the doctor placed her hand over her mouth and stared at Rena. "You're a vegan. You told me you've been one all your life."

"I know. My mother was a very devout ethical vegan during my upbringing and I've carried on in veganism on my own. Ecstatic to do so."

Dr. Jung-tu frowned.

"What!" Rena called out at her silence then rushed on, "Look, I went to the local seafood restaurant three times. It was like if I didn't get the salmon I'd go out of my mind. I ordered the food, paid and left without eating it."

Lowering her hand, Dr. Jung-tu commented, "I'm sure it would have made you ill, never having had meat before, especially with your current situation."

"At this point, why do I care if I get sick?" Rena called out vehemently.

Her doctor sighed. "I know this has been a difficult time for you. However, there are other ways to get what your body maybe lacking. As you know spinach, asparagus, broccoli, collards, watercress and tofu are very high in iron and protein."

She made a dry laugh. "I tried those. The sickness still stayed and so did the craving." Shaking her head, she asked, "How do you crave something you've never eaten before?"

"Any irritability?"

"Some."

"However, that could be due to the ill feeling."

Rena shrugged a shoulder.

"Racing heart?"

"No."

"Exhaustion?"

"Nope. I lay down because I'm sick, but I'm not overly tired."

Dr. Jung-tu scanned Rena's face and skin more closely as if looking for something. "Stick out your tongue."

Complying, Rena opened her mouth wide as her doctor stood and shined the light in her mouth.

"Not swollen. With the seafood cravings, any dirt, corn starch or other unusual substances?"

Rena could feel her face scrunch and tighten, "Who would eat...?" She shook the gross thought away and tried to stay focused on her own issue. "Nothing like that but..."

"But...?"

"The honey."

"What about it?" The doctor flipped the record over

and read through the documentation sent from Rena's pediatrician. "It states you're severely allergic to it. If you had some that may—"

"No, no. I didn't but I wanted to. I've continued with agave nectar as is the vegan norm. However, more than I wanted the meat the honey has driven me almost insane. Last night I found myself at the all-night superstore standing in the aisle before all those jars and bottles of various types of honey. I couldn't even recall getting in my car and driving there."

Returning to the stool, Dr. Jung-tu mumbled, "This is very strange."

"You're telling me. I stood there sweating, shaking, salivating, and practically drooling on myself like an imbecile. I was so freaked out I ran from the store."

"I believe in some holistic treatments and with all of your stomach ailments I would have suggested adding honey to your diet, but not with the extreme allergies your childhood doctor annotated. So, it is unusual for you to desire it."

"It is. Please check the iron levels."

"I will add some more blood tests to see what is going on." Swiveling around in her small, squeaky, black stool again, the doctor turned her computer. "I already have your iron from the two times we've pulled your blood." Tapping away at the keys she called up the information. "You first set of labs taken two weeks ago are completely normal, slightly low on the next, but good range still." Clicking away again, she continued. "Comparing the results to this week may show us something." There was more tapping and clicking.

The doctor added in some notations to her notes, then turned. "The results should be back in a few days then we will see. I changed your medication to something a lot stronger. Zofran. It will definitely take away the nausea. It may make you a little tired so stay active at work."

Smiling, Rena felt relieved. She didn't care if she gave her an elephant tranquilizer as long as the sick feeling deep in the pit of her stomach went away. "Thanks. Should I start taking an over-the-counter iron supplement?"

Standing, Dr. Jung-tu shook her head. "Since your levels were not that low, due to your natural food diet, I would hold off. You don't want too high iron either." The doctor's mouth bowed up as she comforted her with words. "Don't worry, we will figure it out. If I can't, I'll send you to a specialist."

"Great," Rena groaned. More doctors–that was all she needed.

"I will call you with the results. Try not to worry until then. Pick your medicine up at the pharmacy. It will be ready when you finish dressing."

"Thanks, Dr. Jung-tu."

Nodding, the doctor stepped out, pulling the door behind her.

Dropping her head in her hands, Rena wanted to scream. After months of dealing with this weird illness, she was mentally exhausted. She'd hoped in coming to see her doctor this time there would have been more answers and less questions.

Getting dressed, she put all of her hope in the new medication. It was stronger, the doctor had said, and she would be happy with the peace *and* rest it would bring her. Picking up her meds, she got into her car and headed home.

~YH~

There was no breeze blowing that night, but it felt cooler than the air in her house. Inside, Rena felt stifled, unable to breath and ill. Being outside at night was slightly calming, not by much, but she no longer tossed and turned in her lonely bed. Her body was still off balance and her stomach turned worse with the new medication than before. It seemed the stronger the meds her doctor prescribed for her, the more intense her negative reaction to them. Sitting on her back patio, on the third floor of a posh high-rise over top of a city center shopping area, she stared into the sky. The crescent-shaped moon appeared so small in the city. Too many tall buildings seemed to clutter the view. The city lights made the moon look dull and insignificant.

Rena didn't know why that bothered her tonight, but it did. Everything was annoying her suddenly. In a few hours she had to be at work. She worked from four in the morning to one in the afternoon as an assistant producer on a local kids network. They brought fairy tales to life for children. She'd been with the company for seven years. She had interned with them during college, gotten a permanent position soon after, and moved up from a gofer's helper to assistant producer. Her life had seemed perfect, because her career was on a steady rise, until two months ago. Now she got a lot of raised eyebrows and groans from her boss. Not to mention the station manager was starting to pretend she didn't exist. Those were not good signs.

Going inside, she grabbed a light blanket from the couch and curled up on the wicker lounge and attempted to block out the sounds of traffic and the occasional siren. She had to get some sleep and hope that she'd have enough strength and energy for the day at work.

~YH~

"Son, you're in your third season since you returned home from your wandering years. It is time for you to choose a mate. The time is now."

Corduroy Bjorn stretched out beside the lake with his hand in the water and listened to his father, Jasper. He didn't have to turn his head to know his father's face was etched with concern. His features had held that expression for weeks now. Most of the male bears in Den County had just returned from a county line run. A couple weeks away from the First Frost Moon had everyone on edge. It was now past midnight. Frogs and other woodland creatures called out to their mates. Cord understood that he would soon be thirty-three. Most of his friends had paired up within the last two years, but they had no problem finding their life mates. Hell, even his friend Theo, who had begun his wandering journey with him, at the last festival had claimed his second life mate—a human female who had been blessed with the Great Spirit. All others had found mates within the community. However, Cord knew deep within that his mate was not in the county.

"I wish it was that easy." Cord turned his head and looked at his father who lay unashamed and nude with his back propped against the base of a tree. At sixty-two his father was still a physically fit man. Cord knew it was because of their genetic make-up that his father would never diminish in bulk, strength, agility or lose muscle tone as his temples grayed.

Sighing, his father pierced him with an onyx-eyed stare, a mirror of his own as well as the rest of the Were-bears in Den. "You *have* to make it that easy son. If you have not chosen on the night of the First Frost

Moon, the next day during the life mate ceremony I will make sure it's done."

Facing the water again, Cord rolled up to a seated position barely mindful of the debris clinging to his own sweat-coated form. His mind played images of the available women in their community. Beautiful Were-females, who were fertile and ready to find a male to commit themselves to for life, females who didn't stir his heart or his lust. Even his ex was easily discarded. Each one passed through his thoughts in a haze until he reached the only female that had captured every part of him, long ago. He knew she was a woman now, but he could only picture her as a teenage girl, the last time he'd seen her. At almost sixteen, he had already been two years into his first season. However, his mating lust had not fully activated yet.

A group of them had been out fishing and swimming that day. He'd taught her how to fish all afternoon and she'd struggled with the line and hook, getting it caught on everything but in a fish's mouth. He had visions of teaching her to salmon catch while in bear form as the delicious fish swam upstream to mate. He'd been shocked when the girl had told him that her parents never allowed her to fish or taste of the iron-enriched treat.

She'd laughed along with everyone as they joked around about her poor technique. She'd been over two years younger than he. But, she'd still intrigued him with her natural ebony waves in a wild array surrounding her face, her full lips and her skin, brown as if kissed at birth by the sun. When she'd finally caught a fish, her hazel eyes had shimmered with pride. Sitting on the short pier beside her, he'd been unable to resist. Leaning in he'd kissed her. It was an action done on pure instinct. He didn't stop to consider the others around them swimming, talking and fishing. It didn't matter what anyone else thought, whether they saw them.

At that moment, he had to taste her. The kiss had been sweet in the beginning, his lips against hers but an impulse to slip his tongue between her lips changed everything. The contact of their tongues felt as if he'd been shocked by a lightning bolt, causing them both to pause and in that small window of time, he felt her heartbeat. His body seemed to come alive for the first time during that kiss. As a Were, he was ultra sensitive and intensely he felt everything—the inside of her mouth was warm, it throbbed and pulsed, matching rhythm with his. She had been the first to pull away, shy and nervous. Her hand had covered her lips as if trying to control the pulsation; he'd had the same urge. It hadn't been his first kiss, but he was positive it was hers. Then everything had changed in an instant.

She was gone. Taken away by her mother and he'd never seen her again. Since then, he'd kissed other girls and women, expecting the same result and never finding it. There had been no electric current shooting through his body and the only pulsing he'd felt was in his lap. None of the other women's heartbeats could he feel unless he reached out and touched their pulse points with his hand. The final disappointment had been his onyx eyes had never become gold again.

"Is it wrong of me to request time to find a partner like you have with mom? A match. Someone whose heart shadows my own?" Glancing away from the shimmering water, he captured his father with a stare.

His father shook his head and dragged his fingers through his short hair. "No, son it is not. However, time is running down. You're the next in line to lead the sleuth, mayor of Den, but you cannot do that if you are not equipped in all areas. Tim will attempt to sway the county. My brother's son has a silver tongue and will begin to pull the community in his direction."

A low growl rumbled in Cord's chest. "We both know I am stronger than Tim. I have bested him several time—"

The hand his father raised stopped him.

"But he has found his companion, *his life mate*. Last year, while you were not around...when you left." His father shook his head, still disappointed by Cord's actions. "Now, you will begin to see that their joining will provide Tim the strength and leadership he will need. Nita even now is breeding and even that will add to it. As I have told you before, you and your twin sisters gave me great might. I used it to guide the community, not abuse and force them as Artie would have done." His father sighed and stared up at the stars and the moon. "Now, Tim will desire it from you. It is how my brother has raised him."

Cord sat silently, just like his father; he cast his gaze toward the heavens, the moon. More than half of it was not visible yet. However, he knew, could sense his time was running out. He would have to choose. All that his father said was correct. His uncle Artie had envied his older brother, Cord's father, all their lives. Artie had raised Tim with the passion to be mayor of Den.

Did he want the line to be altered because of him? Cord knew deep in his soul that was not the case. His great-grandfather had led the first sleuth of Were-bears into the Redwood Forest in northern California; first to conceal them from humans that would have hunted them down and second to unite them all in one place.

Lorek Bjorn built a community and it had thrived under his leadership. That mantle was passed at sixty to the first male son.

"Maybe it is best if Tim takes the community when you step down next year. If I don't find my real companion, my strength will not increase anyway."

The warm presence of his father kneeling beside him and the firm hand on his shoulder made Cord look at the older man. The leader of the community.

"Then whichever Were-female you choose, you mate with her fiercely and often. Ensure she is breeding soon and that child will still fortify you. Besides you have my first-born bloodline and that of every Bjorn leader before me so that means you have more strength in your core naturally than Tim could have with five cubs."

His father's mouth pulled up on one side. It wasn't a complete smile, but one Cord understood was meant to encourage him. He'd seen it several times over the last few months.

"I won't disappoint, Dad." Cord covered his father's hand with his.

The smile stretched wide this time. "I never thought you would. Now, let's go for a swim and get home before your mother sends Mina and Kelly after us."

"Oh, Great Spirit, I ho—"

Before Cord could finish his sentence the cool water of the lake surrounded him, a result of his father giving him a shove into the water. Cord broke through the surface sputtering, eyeing his father who was still standing on the bank clutching his stomach chuckling. "Fine old man, if you think that's funny, watch me beat you to the Berend pier."

Jasper Bjorn's expression sobered, as he yelled.

"You cheat."

"I didn't give *myself* a head start." Cord called back as he began swimming in the direction of the pier a little under a half-mile away.

There were multiple splashes behind him as not only his father but other males joined the race. Weres were naturally competitive and couldn't resist a challenge no matter the reason it had been issued.

This was just what Cord needed to take his mind off finding a life mate. Correction, only a companion. At least for a little while he had the pleasure of focusing on nothing but his strokes slicing through the water.

When the pseudo race had ended, Cord was the victor with his father only a single stroke behind him followed by other Den County males falling in. Cord pulled himself onto the pier and sat on the end, staring into the water at the other men looking up at him. Apprehension cloaked his shoulders for a moment. *Can I lead them? Am I the* right *person to lead them?*

A Bjorn male had never taken the seat of mayor without a life mate, that additional strength now his father expected it of him.

Tilting his head back he stared up into the night sky. The crescent-shaped moon hung high above his head. Cord wanted to send up a prayer to the Great Spirit, but he wasn't even sure what to pray for: guidance? wisdom? patience? All of those were probably appropriate but there was only one thing his gut wanted him to entreat the Spirit for, but he doubted it was even an option.

CHAPTER TWO

Rena sat at her desk, feeling green. Her stomach felt like a pitbull had his jaws locked around it and was shaking the rest of her like a ragdoll. She was so off balance that bile had taken up residence in the back of her throat for hours and was now staging another escape from her stomach. That morning, she had not consumed another anti-nausea pill, not after last night's prayer at the toilet. Sitting before her computer she tried to concentrate on the data collected on the previous show season, but the image before her was coming in and out of focus with each wave of queasiness. She didn't want to be at work and she couldn't afford to go home again. Not if she wanted to keep her job. As soon as she could take a break she was calling her doctor and attempting a lunch-hour appointment.

"We need to talk, Rena." A firm, light voice spoke to her from the side.

Rena hadn't even heard her supervisor

approaching. Glancing up, she stared at the older black woman, with her designer glasses and long Nubian braids, standing at the opening of her cubicle. "Good morning, Ms. Crawford." Rena forced a smile on her lips and attempted to lace her voice with cheer.

"It doesn't look so good for you." Sighing, her supervisor continued, "My office please." Turning on the four-inch burgundy heels that complimented the dark gray suit she wore, Ms. Crawford strutted away.

Picking up her ginger ale, Rena took a liberal gulp of the soda, hoping it would calm her stomach, then rose and followed her boss.

"Take a seat, please." Ms. Crawford moved behind her desk and directed Rena to one of the two chairs beside it.

Claiming one, Rena waited as her supervisor stared at her. The other woman assessed her slowly, looking from her face — that Rena knew was showing beads of sweat — to the hand that clutched at the clothing over her stomach and finally arriving at Rena's flats that were anxiously tapping against the carpet. Rena had given up wearing heels weeks ago as her sickness had increased. It was bad enough trying to maintain balance standing, let alone fearing she'd topple over three extra inches from the ground.

"You look terrible." Ms. Crawford's voice was direct and calm, a touch of sympathy echoed behind it.

"I'm okay." Rena lied.

"No, Rena you're not. You look a mess. Your work hasn't been getting done for weeks and what you do turn in is so below your expert status, it's laughable."

Those words hurt, even though Rena knew they were the truth. "I'll do better. I'll come in early and stay late if I have to, so I can get things done right." She could hear the whining in her own voice, but she didn't want to lose her job and she could almost sense the hammer coming down.

"When, Rena? In between doctor appointments?" Ms. Crawford threw her hands up in a helpless gesture. "You have no more sick time remaining. Another boss would have canned you months ago. But I like you, and over the years you have kicked ass here. But—"

"Don't say it." Gripping the arm of the chair, Rena rushed on, "I can do this. I know I can. Green or not, I can do this job better than most people in this department." She wasn't bragging but telling the truth. She had a cubicle filled with awards from the station.

Leaning forward, Ms. Crawford barked out, "No, Rena, you're better than every fucking person I supervise on the production staff and that is the only reason that once you get yourself better I'll hire you back in an instant. I'll create a job for you if it comes to it." In low tones, she finished, "But, now I have to let you go."

Rena could feel the burning in her eyes and the tears crawling down her cheeks. Nodding, she stood and headed toward the door. There was nothing else that needed to be said.

"Get better, Rena." It was almost a command, an order from a supervisor to an employee.

Pausing in stride, Rena glanced over her shoulder and took in the smooth sophisticated woman that had trained her and been a good mentor. "I will."

Continuing on, she went to her cubicle, packed up her things in an old box she'd found and left the building, not stopping to say goodbye to anyone.

~YH~

"Hi, Grandma. What are you doing at the Sheriff's office at this time of night?" Lying on the cement slab of her balcony patio again, Rena pressed her cell phone to her ear. She was thankful she'd had the foresight to bring it out with her. She was happy it was her grandmother calling her, not her mom. Her mother, Lillian, was the type of parent that called at odd times of the day and night. Most people would call it nosy or controlling, and so would Rena, but she also knew her mother cared and was always concerned. Especially since Rena first became ill. Her mother had encouraged her to go to the physician but also warned Rena about her allergies.

Rena had not opened up to her mother fully. She'd not confessed her cravings and maddening desire for those forbidden items and something else, something she could not completely express to herself or others. She was hearing voices. More like a voice. Not around her but inside of her. So low, Rena couldn't make out the words.

"It's not that late in California."

"That was true." Rena had momentarily forgotten that it was late in North Carolina where she lived but three hours earlier at her grandmother's house.

"What's wrong, Red dear?"

Feeling as if she wanted to cry from the overwhelming ache in her stomach, and the calm comfort of her grandmother using her nickname, Rena inhaled a few breaths and took in the cool night air. She was no weakling and hated that her illness had brought her down to this.

"I'm okay, Grandma."

"Now, Red, don't you lie to me." Genma Berend admonished, the firmness of her statement coming through the line. "I can hear it in your voice that you are not well."

Her grandmother was always astute, wise and practically clairvoyant if Rena had to put a name on it. With a dry, low laugh, Rena said, "I don't want you to worry."

"Let me take care of my own emotions. What's going on?"

Rena's heavy sigh shot into the air. Her grandmother had always been her private confidant. Her mother didn't realize how often she and her grandmother still communicated. Rena's mother and grandmother had a falling out when Rena was younger and it had been since that time that Rena had seen her grandmother. However, Rena would still go to the park at least twice a month and call her grandmother. She never asked what the disagreement was concerning, and neither of the two women seemed to want to volunteer the information. Her grandmother would always just say, it is your mother's concerns and not mine to share.

Rena knew better than to ask her mother. The spring after her mother had taken her away, Rena had asked to go see her grandmother. However, her mother had become angry and told her that her grandmother's county was not 'safe' for Rena. Not a healthy place for a young girl to be raised.

She found it hard to believe since her mother had lived in that wooded community all her life, so Rena just let the conversation die.

"I'm not well, grandmother."

"That I can hear." Genma was always straight and to the point. "Have you seen a doctor?"

"I have. My physician and I have tried many things

over the past year."

"A year!" The outrage in her grandmother's voice was more than clear. "Why haven't you said anything before?"

"I did—"

"Don't you dare say you didn't want me to be bothered."

Rolling to her back, Rena closed her eyes and just tried to absorb the light breeze moving that night. "I wasn't. I was going to say that I thought it was a passing thing. I didn't think that almost a year later I'd still have no answers. It's called *modern* medicine for crying out loud."

"But they still don't know shit."

"Grandmother!" Rena laughed and groaned, feeling the ache increase as her stomach clenched.

"It's the truth. Tell me what is going on. What are your symptoms? Maybe I can send you something in the mail."

Rena didn't doubt that her grandmother at the moment was taking notes on the various jars of herbs she grew and stocked. In the background she could hear the low hum of radio that she knew was in the sheriff's office from many other calls she'd had with her grandmother. Den County was deep in the woods of Northern California. All of the residents there communicated through CB radios.

"Nausea like I'm going to throw up or pass out at any moment. Which I've done both more times than I can count."

"Hm hmm...what else?" She imagined her grandmother scratching fiercely on a tablet.

"Nothing real." Moving her hand to her stomach Rena rubbed it mindlessly. "We've tried pills and various medicines…I even went to see an acupuncture therapist. That was a joke. She just told me some mumbo jumbo about my life about to change…or transition…or shift… I can't remember."

The other end of the line went silent. "Shift? You said she said shift?"

Shaking her head, Rena recalled that frustrating day of finally reaching out to a woman that a coworker had told her helped her to stop smoking. However, the woman didn't do a thing for Rena and afterward her symptoms even seemed to get worse.

"Something like that. But I'm sure she was indicating that I was going to lose my job. Standing in the unemployment line is one major transition she could have warned me about."

"Sorry about your job. I know it was something you really enjoyed."

"I did, but I'm more concerned about getting myself better. I have enough savings to get by for a while."

"Red, are you sure sweetheart that nothing else is going on? That you've had no other symptoms?"

She wondered what her grandmother had cooking in her mind. Genma never asked any arbitrary questions. "No, just the nausea that usually brings on a headache and full body aching. Reason I thought it was just a bad case of the flu."

"I see. Anything strange happen?"

Strange? Rena pushed herself up to a sitting position. The hair on her arms rose and there was a tingling sensation along her spine. Did my grandmother know something about what was going on with me? "Grandmother, do we have a family history of some kind of illness? I tried to ask mother, but she just shooed me off the topic and simply instructed me to stick to my diet."

"That diet is ridiculous. No fish, no honey… who has ever heard of anything so ridiculous. What kind of vegetarian is she trying to be?" Her grandmother went off on a rant about her mother and Lillian Hoodman's rearing style.

Rena knew that just like when her mother went off about her grandmother this could go on for almost an hour.

"Well, you know I'm allergic to those things, grandmother."

"Allergic. Hm. Maybe you should have *your* doctor retest you."

Laughing at the heavy attitude in her grandmother's voice, Rena said, "You may have a point. Especially in the last month or so I've been having a craving for both of them. Particularly honey."

Just saying the word made her mouth salivate and images of the golden syrup flash into her mind. Her hand around the phone began to shake. She switched hands and took a deep, steadying breath. *It will pass. It will pass.*

"Red sweetie, did you say you've been craving fish and honey?"

Rolling her bottom lip between her teeth, she licked it and her mind tried to imagine the taste of it — honey.

"Yes, ma'am." Her throat was tight making the words come out high and squeaky.

"Hmm hm. Look, dear, since you have time off now, why don't you come here?"

"Oh, that would be nice. But, all I can do for the most part is lay around. You're so active, Grandma, I don't want to be in your way or slow you down."

"Nonsense. That was the reason for my call. I will

be away from home for a few days and I need someone to keep an eye on my house."

"You live in the middle of the woods. Have you been having trouble with people coming around...bothering you?" Rena's body was on full alert. Her grandmother was extremely vital for a woman of her eighty plus years, but Rena still worried about her.

"Oh, no one's stupid enough to be in Den County where they don't belong. Not without great risk," Genma declared. "Anywho. I have a landscaper coming to do something around the house. So, it's really about having someone let him in or tell him where I want things. Come on and help your old granny out."

Not caring about the pain it caused her, Rena let out a loud laugh. "Grandma, you have *never* been old."

"That's true and I don't plan to ever be." Her grandmother's robust chuckle flooded the line. "What do you say?"

Pulling her legs to her chest, Rena stared through the rails of her porch and considered her options.

"I really think the woodland air will do your body good. I'll bake you a batch of my famous muffins. People love them here."

"Now you're just playing dirt. But it worked."

"It always does. When can you come?"

"You're the one taking a trip. When do you leave?" Getting up, Rena went back into her apartment. Leaving the patio door open, she went to the couch and sat.

"On Monday. Can you be here Sunday?"

"I'll be there."

"Excellent. I'll get everything set for your arrival." If

it was possible, her grandmother's voice was filled with even more vigor.

"Please don't go through too much trouble."

"You just keep yourself healthy enough to make it here. I'll handle the rest."

Smiling, Rena, was getting excited too about the trip. It had been way too many years since she'd seen her grandmother. Mostly because of her mother's wishes, but also because of distance, Rena's schooling and trying to excel at her job. Now, she hated that she'd given so much of her time to her career only to have it disappear.

"You got it. I love you."

"I love you, too, Red. Call me once you have your flight arrangements. I'll pick you up from the airport."

"I can just take a cab to your house, Grandma."

"See that proves you have been away for way too long. A cab will not come this distance nor be allowed into Den County at that time," her grandmother declared.

Frowning, Rena asked, "Not allowed?"

"Don't worry about it. Talk to you soon, dear."

"Grand—" Rena held the dead phone away from her face, shocked at how fast her grandmother rushed from the phone.

Shrugging it off, she set her cell on the table and curled up on the couch. As she pulled the throw blanket up over her body she admitted that she felt a little better with the plans to visit her grandmother. Even though physically she was still ill, emotionally she felt bolstered and recharged.

Closing her eyes, her last thought as she drifted off to sleep was...*Maybe things will be better for me after this trip to Den.*

~YH~

"I'll have a big bowl of your famous stew, Ann." Cord leaned back in the booth seat and smiled up at Ann Gobi, his good friend Theo's aunt.

Ann and her husband Paul owned Gobi's Diner. It was the only home-style eatery in town.

"You got it. I'll get you some bread out here, too. A growing man needs all his nourishment with the coming week ahead."

"Bring me some of your wonderful sweet butter to slather on the bread while you're at it, please."

"I sure will." She winked at him and moved toward the kitchen.

He turned and stared out the window. There really wasn't any need for anyone to remind him that the First Frost Moon was coming up. Everyone in town was abuzz about it. People were already moving stands and tents into the field on the far end of the park. It was the most exciting time in Den for all residents.

On Sunday, his father, as the mayor of Den, would be making a speech officially closing down Den for the week of the festival. There would be games, shows, cookouts, family picnics and people selling various foods and items that they had made during the year. All of it just celebrated who they were as Weres.

There were not many visitors to Den, but blocking off all the outside roads that led to town kept anyone from 'happening by'. He chuckled to himself as he thought about how the cinderblocks had not been a barrier to Theo's mate ending up in their town. Presently his friend and his family were out of town visiting Theo's mate Riley's family.

Through the diner window, he watched all the

families and couples moving about the town and felt a deep ache in his gut. They appeared happy and content, as the male and female Were-bears made eyes at each other or walked with arms linked as kids followed behind. This week, the festival, was all leading up to one thing–the Bear Run. It happened the last night of the festival. All of the eligible female and male Weres ran through the woods in hopes of finding their life mate. The females would scatter through the forest and the males would give chase, allowing their noses and hearts to lead them by the scent of the one the Great Spirit meant for them.

Rarely was there ever a mistake. Rarely was there a Were-bear who just selected one that was available without the soul tie. However, that would be the case for him. He wasn't looking forward to it.

"Hey, Cord."

He picked up on her scent before she'd spoken. Hibiscus. That's what Marcella's smell reminded him of. The floral woodsy aroma wasn't offensive, just notable. Since she was frequently around, he picked up on it quite often.

"Marcella. How's your day going?" He brought his gaze around to her. At five-five with a small frame and dark brown straight hair, the Asian woman was a small brown bear, but one of the quickest females in town.

Her cheeks tinted, but she didn't take her eyes off him. "Very well now. You mind if I join you or are you expecting company?"

He didn't want to encourage her. He knew she was interested in him. Over the years since he'd returned from his wandering time, she'd let him know that she was available and attracted to him. They'd messed around a few times in the past, but for him there hadn't been any connection. During the last time, she'd asked him to bite her and it had been like a bucket of ice water tossed in his face.

Not yours. His bear had screamed within him.

After that encounter, he'd let her know that he wasn't ready for a commitment yet and she should consider that being around him might be keeping her life mate away. Last run he'd gone away for a month surrounding the festival hoping she'd participate and someone would claim her. No such luck.

"Not expecting anyone. Just came in for a quick lunch." He owned Digging Deep Landscaping, even though his warehouse was in town, he spent most of his time working on jobs with his crew. When he was able to get a meal in at Gobi's it made his week. However, it made avoiding Were's he preferred to stay away from a little more difficult. Like Marcella.

Sliding into the seat on the other side of the booth, she gave him a small smile as she beguilingly tilted her head. "I'll just keep you company."

"If you want."

"So, are you looking forward to —"

"Here you go, Cord. A nice steaming bowl of soup, warm bread and lots of honey-sweetened butter." Ann's timing was perfect as she came to the table and placed the food before him.

"Ah, Ann, you steal my heart. I do believe I'd starve if not for you."

Swatting his arm, the older woman laughed. "All you Den males are such charmers. You know your momma taught you well."

"That she did," Cord agreed. Eating was something that Were-bears loved and with the winters being so heavy in the area, everyone learned young how to cook.

"Can I get you anything, Marcella?" Ann turned to the younger woman.

Cord could only imagine what Ann was thinking. Everyone in Den probably expected that he'd choose Marcella during the run. The only person that didn't agree was his bear.

"No, thanks, Ann. I'm fine," Marcella said.

"Alright, let me know if you change your mind." Ann moved back to her place behind the counter.

"How's the salon going?" Cord wanted to get her on another topic before she journeyed back to the one about the festival. Tearing off some bread, he smeared a healthy amount of butter on it before dipping it into the salmon chowder soup then placing it in his mouth.

"Good. Real good. Mama actually listened to some of my ideas about it. In the spring she's going to have Theo start on a second floor where I can begin some of the treatments and spa services."

"Well, that's great. I know how important that is to you, being able to use your massage therapy degree."

"It is." Her dark brown eyes lit up. "I'm glad you remember."

Oh, shit. Did I make a mistake? "Of course. I try and recall those things about my *friends* that they hold dear." Spooning the thick, creamy soup into his mouth, he hoped she'd picked up on his emphasis on friend.

Stretching her hand across the table, she cupped the back of his hand that was holding another piece of bread.

He could feel the heat in her hand, but other than that his body had no response. Not even a residual bubble of lust from their past.

"I was hoping that we could be more than friends again, Cord. I've never gotten—"

Dropping his chin to his chest, he took a deep breath and sighed heavily. "Marcella. I don't want to lead you on. I can't make any promises about Friday night."

"I'm not expecting you to. I just want you to know that I'm more than willing to be—"

"Cord, there you are!" Genma Berend came bustling into the diner with all the energy and vigor she always had. Beside her was her partner in crime, Octavia Bjorn, his grandmother.

Thankful for the timely interruption, Cord set his spoon down, moved his hand from beneath Marcella's and rose to greet the two older women.

"Nana." He kissed his grandmother's cheek first then her best friend's. "Ms. Genma."

"I went by your business and Rand said you were here." Genma prattled on.

"What can I help you with?" he looked from one to the other.

His grandmother looked pointedly at Marcella, then him. He couldn't read her expression, he hoped that she wasn't about hassle him like the rest of the town was over choosing Marcella.

"We're not disturbing anything are we? You don't mind excusing us do you, dear? I see you don't have anything to eat or drink, I assume you were just briefly stopping by." Octavia was anything but subtle even with the wide grin on her mouth.

Apparently, his grandmother figured whatever she and Genma had to discuss with him was more important than what Marcella was talking about.

"We don't want to hold you. I know how busy the

salon can be at lunchtime. Especially with the festival coming up next week." Genma gave Marcella a sweet smile.

Cord feared that if Marcella didn't leave soon the two older Were-females would shift and bodily move her from the seat.

"I do need to get back." Rising, Marcella looked at him, a cloud of emotions shadowing her eyes as if she were attempting to communicate something with him. "Cord, I'll see you later, so we can finish our talk."

"Take care, Marcella." He shook his head as he saw the female walk away, swaying her hips. It would probably take an act of the Great Spirit to get her to see there was no future for them.

Once the two precocious ladies had taken up the seat Marcella had vacated, he sat and resumed eating. He knew his grandmother and Genma wouldn't need any prompting to speak.

"Cordy-bear—"

"Nanaaa…" he growled, at thirty plus moons old, his grandmother still wouldn't stop calling him by his childhood nickname.

"Okay, okay. Sweetheart, you know that since Genma and I don't have any grandcubs…" She allowed those words to hang in the air.

Genma lowered her head and shook it slowly as if the thought of her not having small ones to spoil was depressing.

Biting a healthy piece of bread, he rolled his eyes. This must be good if they were starting with a guilt trip.

"We've decided to go away for a few days this week," Octavia continued.

"Nana, everyone loves your wicker baskets. You're

not going to sell them this year during the festival?"

"Your sisters have agreed, since they have another year before they can participate in the run, they will man my Bjorn Basket tent."

He chuckled as he lifted his glass of honeyed tea and took a swallow. His sisters were all about the festival events and making sure they riled up all the Were-males their age, flirting. It was doubtful that the two girls volunteered willingly. However, he knew better than to contradict his grandmother.

"Lola Shardik has agreed to sell my muffins with her honeycombs," Genma explained. "So, no one will even miss us."

"Not likely," he commented and pushed his empty bowl to the side. "What do you all need from me?"

His grandmother looked at Genma and Genma returned the look. It was full of secrets and a deeper level of communication. If they were Were-male and female, he would have believed they had a mindlink going on.

Pulling a napkin out from the dispenser he wiped his mouth, using the moment to cover his smirk.

"I need some repairs around my house. Odds and end things done to my yard," Genma explained. "Winter flowers planted."

"Not forgetting the re-soiling and fertilizing of your garden for those awesome winter vegetables," Octavia added.

Genma looked at her and smiled. "Oh, thank you. This year I'll probably plant beets, carrots, some parsnip, maybe fava beans and brussel spr—"

"Ladies... ladies, can we please get to what you need?" Cord ran his hand over his head, knowing that these two ladies were anything but tangential.

Everything they did had a plan and purpose. They were too sharp-witted for normal elderly babbling.

"Sorry, dear." His grandmother reached across the table and patted his hand. "Anywho. We were wondering if you could take care of it while we were gone."

"During the festival week?" For a moment he was willing to take back all his thoughts about these two women being incisive.

"I know it's a no work week, but it would really mean a lot to me to have it done. Then I can start my planting when I return." Genma took hold of his other hand.

Looking from one woman to the other, one black with a short silver twist in her hair and the other white with wheat blonde locks cut in a bob below her chin, as they gave him puppy dog eyes, Cord shook his head. Pleading eyes from these two meant trouble.

Unable to refuse them anything, he nodded. "Fine. Fine. I'll take care of it. I wasn't planning to do much around the festival anyway."

"Fit it in when you can." Genma patted him then moved her hand away. "I'll have lots of muffins inside for you. Heavy on the honey-glaze, right?"

He cocked a smile at his grandmother's best friend. Genma knew him too well. "Yes, ma'am."

Their job done, his grandmother slid from the bench first, followed by Genma.

Needing to get back to work, he rose as well. After tossing cash down on the table for the meal and tip, he escorted the two scheming ladies out of the diner.

"Thanks again, dear. I knew I could count on you." Octavia stepped to him and kissed him on the cheek. She didn't immediately step away, but cupped his face, her gaze full of sincerity as she said, "Soon, life will look up for you. I just know it will. Don't fret."

Staring into deep set, coal eyes that mirrored his own, he took her words to heart. "If you say so, Nana, I believe it."

Giving her a quick kiss on the top of her head, he turned and left the two best friends on the sidewalk. Crossing the road he headed to his truck wanting to get back to work. He'd had enough of the women in his life for the rest of the afternoon..

CHAPTER THREE

"Grandma, I forgot how beautiful your home is."
Rena closed the door to her grandmother's wagon-
style sedan. Taking a moment, she looked around and
just allowed herself to absorb the pure, crisp natural
air.

"Ah, it's nothing. Just my little slice of heaven, that's
all." Her grandmother, still a statuesque woman for
almost eighty, came around the front of the car.

Turning, Rena smiled at her. "It's more than that."
Sliding her arm around her grandmother's shoulder,
she said, "I'm sorry I've stayed away for so long."

Wrapping her thin, but strong, arm around her
waist, her grandmother squeezed her tight. "Don't be.
Everything happens in its timing."

"True. I'm still ashamed that I let my mother's
wishes keep me from yo—"

Swatting her on the hip, Genma stepped away. "Oh,
pooh. It's not like I'm going to kick my toes up anytime
soon." Chuckling, she went to the back hatch of the

vehicle and opened it.

Shaking her head, Rena followed her to the rear of the wagon, gravel shifting and grinding beneath her feet. "Grandma, you're going to hurt yourself. Get the smaller one. I can get the big suitcase." She reached out to claim the bag from her grandmother.

Rena was shooed to the side, as Genma walked past her lugging a heavily packed bag as if it didn't weigh more than a handful of groceries.

Reaching in, Genma collected the smaller one in her other hand. "You can barely carry yourself, let alone anything else."

Her grandmother was right, Rena did feel weak. The plane ride from coast to coast had practically done her in. During the two-hour drive from the airport she had slept most of the way, missing all the tranquil scenery. Still feeling queasy, she admired the woman before her with a slack jaw.

"Close your mouth before you catch something." Her grandmother moved toward the house, never breaking stride.

Amazed, Rena lifted her jaw to seal her lips together. She wondered how she could contact the people from the Guiness Book of World Records and get Genma Berend added to it as the world's strongest senior citizen. Rena wondered if over the years, with her grandmother's only child far away and her husband passing away leaving Genma to take care of herself, if that was the reason her grandmother was stronger and more capable than most elderly. Rena wasn't sure about the details surrounding her grandfather's passing. It was something else her mother had refused to talk about.

She never asked her grandmother about it because

she didn't want to bring up something that was hurtful.

Closing the hatch, Rena went to the house. "I can at least unlock the front door for you."

"No need. Why don't you sit on the porch or something? You have plenty of time to get this stuff unpacked and I'll re-familiarize you with the house when you're ready." Her grandmother set the cases down for a moment to open the door then collected them and crossed her threshold. "I'll get us some warm tea."

Country living, Rena thought. In the city where she lived, no one left their homes unlocked, even if they were just going five minutes up the street. It made her wonder once again why her grandmother wanted her here. It was apparent Genma wasn't concerned about a stranger stealing things from her, so it was doubtful Genma would be worried about someone she knew and authorized to be at her house.

Pushing those thoughts away, she took her grandmother's advice and remained outdoors for a moment. The weather here was chillier than in North Carolina. It was fall back at home, but there was only cause for a light sweater at night.

Standing in the great outdoors, she felt too anxious or uneasy to sit. She followed the wraparound porch to the back of the house. Her feet halted at the breathtaking view. Two hundred feet beyond her grandmother's porch was a magnificent lake. The thick trees surrounding the single-level cabin-style home broke just enough for an unobstructed scene of Nature's majesty.

The thick redwoods created the perfect shade no matter which way the sun was shining and the lush grass between the waterfront and the house just made Rena want to take her shoes off and run. Run wild, free and uninhibited by illness. She wanted to feel the wind in her hair and the sun on her face.

"Go on down there if you want to."

Startled, Rena glanced over her shoulder at Genma. "Grandma, I didn't even hear you come out."

Standing at the back door that led to the living room with a tray filled with a porcelain kettle, two cups and what appeared to be a small basket of muffins, her grandmother smiled at her. "You were too focused on getting those shoes off to notice anything."

"What?" Rena looked down and sure enough she had somehow toed herself out of both her shoes. The charcoal grey, Mary Jane-style flats lay skewed in front of her feet, one on top of the other. Laughing, she said, "I didn't even realize I was taking them off."

"Well they're off now, go on out there and feel the grass between your toes. Dip your feet in the lake if you want to." Her grandmother moved to a small table between two rocking chairs and set the tray down.

Glancing away from her grandmother, she squeezed the rough banister beneath her fingers and stared at the sparkling water. "Won't the water be too cold this time of year?"

"For some maybe. But, it won't hurt anything to swing your feet in it. Probably do your constitution well."

Looking back at her grandmother, she asked, "What about the tea? You went to all that trouble to prepare it."

"It will keep." She settled into a rocking chair. "Go on. Everything will be fine."

Clutching the rail again, Rena had a picture flash in

her mind of when she was younger and the other local teens in the area would leap over the banister—agile and free. However, that kind of antics was for children and the healthy. *Not me. Not now.*

Unable to resist the lure, she walked around the side until she reached the steps that led from the kitchen to the yard. She noticed a large area that appeared to be a substantial garden. Presently it was barren, no fruits, flowers or vegetables could be seen. She knew her grandmother had started gardening in the years since Rena and her mother had been gone. Frequently, her grandmother would mail boxes of canned items to her after Rena moved out of her mother's house.

People in the city didn't have gardens and Rena looked forward to feeling better and helping her grandmother plant some things before she returned to the East Coast. Maybe by the time her grandmother got back from whatever trip she was taking.

Walking through the thick grass, she loved hearing the rustling of the blades of grass caused by her steps and feeling the soft, cool prickles too. Rushing to the water, she only had to break her stride a few times because her stomach turned and knotted, but she refused to stop.

The planks of the dock were smooth and warm from the fall sun as her feet slapped against them. Once she arrived at the end of the dock, she sat and leaned against one of the two high beams there.

She closed her eyes, and tried to recall the summers she'd spent right here. However, it was all fuzzy. For too many years her mother wouldn't allow her to talk about Den County, her grandmother or how much she missed it. Lillian Hoodman was having none of that.

"Forget it, Rena. Just leave it alone. Wipe that place

from your memory."

Over and over, for two years following their final departure her mother would repeat the same words.

"I guess you got your wish, mom." Rena opened her eyes, and saw how the expansive lake narrowed downstream and took in the low mountains in the horizon. *New memories*, she told herself.

Testing her grandmother's theory, she lowered her feet from the dock and first dipped her toes then sank to her ankles in the icy water. It was cold, but refreshing in a way she could not understand. Everything in her body began to settle some. The queasy feeling in the pit of her stomach calmed several degrees as she just concentrated on the sensation of the water around her feet and breathed.

When her toes began to feel numb, she pulled them out.

Not wanting to keep her grandmother waiting any longer, Rena rose and followed her earlier path back to the house.

At the house, her grandmother had a towel tossed over the back of the vacant rocker and a shawl beside it. *Did the woman think of everything?*

"Thank you." Rena sat in the seat and dried her feet, rubbing them vigorously until they were warmer. She slipped them back into her shoes that sat neatly at the side of the chair.

"How was the water? Good?"

"Cold." Her teeth did a little chatter, but Rena still let the smile rise. "But good." She wrapped the shawl tightly around her shoulders.

"Here, have a little tea. It's my own special blend." Her grandmother poured her some steaming hot beverage and passed her a cup and saucer.

"Wow, that's some kettle, it is still warm." Rena held the cup up to her face and allowed the steam to remove the slight chill from her skin.

"It's the hot plate." Her grandmother tapped the metal plate below the pot. "Octavia got it for me a few Christmases ago. She and I love sitting out here and watching the snow melt as spring sets in."

"Ah, how is your friend?" Rena recalled numerous phone conversations she'd had with her grandmother about her friend and the things the two women were up to. If someone had overheard their communication they would probably believe Rena was talking to a teenager. Her grandmother went swimming in the lake, out for long hikes, caught salmon with her hands, camped in the mountains and went berry picking.

"Octavia is very excited about going away tomorrow."

"Her family's okay with her leaving on a trip? I remember you telling me she is close to them. Isn't her husband mayor or something?" Rena sipped her tea. It was syrupy sweet just as she liked it. A custom she'd gotten from her mother. She'd watched her mother over the years add extra sugar or agave nectar, saying 'it's never quite sweet enough'.

As if something was missing. However, this cup was perfect. Soon, Rena consumed that one and poured another while her grandmother slowly drank her own.

"Benat previously was mayor… some time ago. Now their son, Jasper, holds the position. Benat doesn't deny Octavia anything that she wishes." A shadow crossed her grandmother's face and Rena wondered if it was brought on by loneliness of her friend having family around her.

Going out on a limb, Rena asked, "Are you thinking about grandpa? I'm sure you miss him. Will you tell me about him?"

Her grandmother sighed, stared off into the distance as she held her teacup steady. "Osborne," she whispered reverently. "He has never left my side." She drank from her cup, and as if it had never been there, the shadow cleared and she smiled as she glanced at Rena. "But that is a conversation better saved for later...perhaps when I return."

Allowing her grandmother the privacy of her own memories, Rena returned her smile. "Then will you at least tell me how much sweetener you used to get this tea so delicious."

"You don't have to add any extra when it is brewed. I cure it when I buy it from the store in town. Simply allow it to bake in the summer sun then store it in a canister."

"You make it sound so simple. I may have to extend my stay just for this. When mom or I do it, it is never quite this tasty. Like something is missing."

"I'm sure. Your mother was raised making my tea when she was younger." Her grandmother exhaled, the sound heavy and strong as she slouched just a little in her chair.

Rena could imagine the weight of the dissension between her and her daughter had worn on her grandmother, even though Genma tried to deny it.

"A lot of things Lillian has pushed aside. Shunning her very nature. The order of things."

Frowning, Rena pondered her grandmother's words. "You mean not being a part of her family? Keeping me from you?"

"That and so much more. There is always time for

such weighted conversation." Lifting the small basket, her grandmother said, "It is more important now to get you rested and well. Have a muffin. They're my sticky-glazed pistachio recipe."

"Oh, Grandma, this tea is working wonders on me, but I think a muffin would be too much." Rena hadn't lied. The tea was having a very soothing effect on her stomach. From the first sip it had warmed her insides and immediately settled the nausea. By the time she completed the first cup she felt more alert and her limbs less shaky. Rena wondered if she consumed the whole pot if she'd be able to run five miles on the treadmill again.

Working out had been one of the first things she'd had to cease almost a year ago. She just didn't have the stamina or energy to get through more than five or ten minutes. Her grandmother should think about selling her recipe to pharmacies and clinics. It was better than anything her doctor had given her.

"Try one and if it causes you to become green about the gills again then you don't have to finish it."

Tilting her head, Rena eyed her grandmother. "How do you know I'm not still feeling as sick as I was when I arrived?"

With a sly smile that curled up on one corner, her grandmother said, "Oh, Red, a grandmother knows." Stretching her arm further, she went on, "Besides, your face has color in it now, not so pale."

Rena was glad to hear that. She got tired of seeing her own ashen brown reflection peering back at her. "Just a bite or two."

Looking at the muffins with their shiny, sticky, nutty topping, Rena couldn't help but lick her lips. She'd always had a sweet tooth and staring at the muffins and trying to decide which one to pick was doing a great job of re-awakening it. Selecting one of the smaller ones from the basket, she took a bite. Like the tea, the first thing she tasted was the sticky sweetness. Her insides seemed to be dancing as she swallowed it. Unable to resist the moist, fluffy goodness and the nut crunch, she took a second and third bite. If it made her sick she would have to deal with it.

"Oh goodness, Grandma, it is soooo good." Rena's eyes rolled up and she leaned back against the rocker. She was in a delectable heaven between the tea and the muffin.

"See, I told you. No one in Den can resist them." Her grandmother chuckled. "Another?"

As the last bite disappeared down her throat, Rena opened her eyes and peeped at her grandmother. "Maybe one more small one. I don't want to push it. It seems like it has been months since I've been able to eat and keep anything down. I'm sure I will pay for this later."

"One never knows." Joining her, her grandmother ate a muffin too. "Tomorrow, Greta from next door will be by to pick up the containers for Lola Shardik that will be sold at the festival next week. They're in a plastic container in my pantry. But, I have a tin in there with your name on it. The other beside it is for the landscaper...he likes his extra sticky."

"Bless you." Rena held the last bite of her second muffin with one hand and picked off the chopped pistachios one at a time, just to prolong the devouring of the last piece. The sappy glaze clung to her fingers. "What is this glaze...cinnamon and brown sugar?"

"All kinds of spices and decadent goodness."

Reaching over, her grandmother placed her hand on top of Rena's and squeezed. "Let's go in, so you can get some rest. I'm sure you're tired."

Popping the last piece into her mouth, Rena licked the sweet residue from her fingers and hands like a child who didn't care. Rising, she collected the tray with all the items on it, before her grandmother could get it. She didn't come here to be waited on hand and foot, something that would make her feel more like a frail invalid.

"I feel fine, Grandma."

"You probably do, but you should lie down for a moment. Not overdo it. Besides, it will give me time to make some nice vegetable chowder for you."

Following her grandmother into the house, Rena moved through the beautifully decorated family room. There was a television mounted on the wooden wall between two tall movie cases. Before it was a long, plush couch and a glider rocker with a foot stool. Out of all the furniture, the glider appeared the most used. Along one wall there was floor-to-ceiling bookshelves, jam packed with books. That was something she knew about her grandmother. She loved to read, especially in the winter months when Den County practically shut down. In the corner in front of the living room window was an easel, a representation of her grandmother's second love, painting. A blank sheet of paper fastened to the top awaited her grandmother next creation.

In the wall across from the bookshelf was a fireplace with logs stacked neatly in a metal box beside it.

Rena had no problem seeing the room filled with children and adults, opening holiday gifts and curled up before a fire. There was a jab of guilt in her heart that her grandmother's life had been so void of family.

Yes, Genma had her friends, but they weren't family and her family had abandoned her. Rena made a promise to herself that her relationship with her grandmother would be different from here on out. There wouldn't just be letters and a monthly phone call. She would visit Genma often. Hopefully, she would get better soon and meet a great guy and fill the remainder of her grandmother's life with grandchildren.

Once they were in the luxurious, fully equipped, modern kitchen, Rena set the tray on the counter. There wasn't a single appliance that she could think of that wasn't in her grandmother's kitchen. Rena was impressed. "Where do you want me to put the rest of the muffins, Grandma?"

"Shoo shoo, Red." Her grandmother flapped her hands up and down in the direction of the entrance that would lead back into the living room. "I can take care of that. Come on, let me show you to your room."

"Okay." Rena laughed at her grandmother's persistence as she followed her back into the main room of the house. She couldn't be mad at Genma because she had come here not only to watch out for her grandmother's house, but also to rest. It was just hard to think about lying down when she was beginning to feel so much better.

"As a refresher to the layout of the house, this is my room." Her grandmother pointed to the first door they passed down a long hallway from the kitchen.

Rena peeped inside and saw the orange and navy blue comforter and decoration in the room. A queen-size bed with a wooden headboard was clearly seen.

The next rooms indicated were across the hall from the master bedroom. They were dual doors that her grandmother told her had a Jack and Jill bathroom between them, a painting of a blue jay on the wall above the towel rack. Both rooms had full-size beds: one brown and green and the other sky blue and white.

"I remember sleeping in the blue and white room, but not the one with colors." Rena stood at the entrance of the room. She could see a budding teenage girl, skinny with long legs and thick unruly hair, lying in the bed. At the same time her memory became flooded with muted words and voices. Her grandmother and mother arguing in the front room. Rena recalled wanting to crack the door and eavesdrop on what was being said, but having no desire to incur her mother's wrath.

"You and mom argued a lot that last summer we were here." Rena looked at her grandmother, now standing before the closed door at the end of the long hall.

Genma's expression was a blank mask. "Lillian and I have butted heads since she was a little girl. She likes to have things her way and she doesn't always understand that there may be a bigger picture she isn't seeing." Falling silent, her grandmother pushed open the other door. "I think you are old enough now to have a more comfortable room."

"It's beautiful, Grandma." Rena walked passed her grandmother still standing at the door. Moving deeper into the room, Rena took in the mango and cream decorations: comforter, piles of pillows, curtains and the large thick area rug under the bed. She noticed that even the bathroom matched the room's color scheme. Her suitcase and carryon were sitting beside the closet.

"I hoped you would like it." When I saw the items last week at the cabin décor shop in town I knew it would be perfect for you.

"Oh, it is. You didn't have to go through all this trouble. I'll only be here a short while."

"Who knows, maybe you will come to love Den as you did when you were younger and stay...longer."

Glancing over at her grandmother, she saw the twinkle in the older woman's eyes.

"No promises." Rena would at least visit more.

"None asked."

Rena sat on the queen-size bed with its thick wood posts. The bed looked as if someone hewed it from a tree and left the bark on it. It was rugged and homey at the same time. The mattress was soft, but firm just like she liked it. "I think I could use a nap on this bed."

"Good. You need your rest. The soup will be ready in a couple of hours. No rush, just rest. I have some final packing to do for my trip."

"I only need a few minutes." Rena slipped her shoes off and curled up on her side, facing the door. A yawn swelled up in her chest and came out louder than she expected. "It's been such a long and agonizing year, Grandma."

Coming to her, Genma grabbed a blanket from the end of the bed and pulled it up over Rena. "Everything will be better soon. Just you wait and see. Things will all start to make sense."

"I hope so. I really do." Physically, she was feeling better, but emotionally, coming back to her grandmother's was draining. Memories were exploding in her mind like popcorn. Fragmented and obscure, it was taking too much mental energy to try and sort out the meaning. Allowing her eyes to slide shut, Rena gave in to her body's wishes and slept.

CHAPTER FOUR

Cord rose from his couch and stretched. The action movie he'd been watching had ended. It was a new release he'd just gotten in the mail. The movie was good and he was looking forward to seeing it a few more times over the winter home hibernation months.

Glancing over at the clock he noted the time. It was getting late and he had a lot of work to do over at Genma's tomorrow. If his father got his wishes, this would be the last landscaping job he took. The position of mayor of Den County was more of a managerial-type job, executed from an office in town next door to the sheriff's office. Cord would have to allow Rand, his assistant manager, to handle the day-to-day operations of his business.

Frustrated, Cord grabbed the now-empty trail mix bowl from the coffee table and took it to the kitchen. Able to see clearly in the dark, he didn't bother to turn on a lamp. Setting it down on the counter beside the sink, he took a moment to stare out into the blackness of night. The glow of the half moon was shining through it and his bear enjoyed being bathed in the light.

Run.

He chuckled at the demands of his bear. Over the last week they'd both become restless. The cause seemed clear to him. *The Bear Run.* There was no way for him to get out of it this year. He had to participate and he had to choose a life mate.

"Shit," the word exploded from his mouth and echoed in the kitchen.

His bear growled. It would be so much easier if his animal side would have claimed Marcella, then he wouldn't be in such torment.

No mate.

The vehemence behind those two words from his bear caused Cord's gut to tighten.

Letting out a heavy sigh, he shoved the Friday night event far into the back of his mind. His bear would have to settle for the choices before them at that time. What they both wanted wasn't possible.

Heading to the back door off the side of his kitchen, Cord stepped into his garage. The smell of soil and floral and plant life greeted him from the bags of fertilizer and seeds stocked in the back of his truck. The scents were always a welcome to him. He loved digging his hands deep into Mother Earth in both bear and human form. He'd miss it.

Getting ready to check the boundaries of his property for the night, he stripped out of his clothes. He moved past his truck and out the open door of his garage. In an instant he took off across his back lawn and with nothing but an image of his bear in his mind he shifted.

Paws pounding on the ground he set out on his nightly excursion. Moving toward the first thick redwood he saw, he pressed his back against it and gave himself a nice deep scratch from the crown of his head to his stubby tail. The bark digging into his spine was like heaven on earth. The only thing better was raw honey from a bee hive.

Dropping back to all fours he continued to trudge on the path, sniffing for anything out of the ordinary. They didn't get many strangers in Den, but it wasn't uncommon for some tree-hugging hiker to venture too far from safer camp grounds. The time or two he'd come across an adventurous camper, a deep loud roar was enough to send them packing. It was normally an entertaining moment for him.

After more than an hour of searching and scenting his property, he continued through the woods that bordered Theo's land. His friend was still away with his family and he kept an eye out on it. Forty-five minutes later, he was still restless and decided to check in on his grandmother's friend. Unlike his grandmother, Genma lived alone with no family close by.

As the mayor, his father normally extended his protection to the single females and elderly in the county.

Moving toward the river, he allowed it to lead him to the widest section, two miles up. His bear was thrilled to be out in the night air longer than usual, feeling the fall breeze in his fur, hearing the mating calls of birds and insects, smelling rich soil and other woodsy scents all around.

There were times Cord wished he could remain in this form. Things were simpler when he was a bear.

As soon as he arrived at the Berend property he saw her. A female bear, sitting in the center of the path that led from the house to the water. As if waiting for something or someone.

He paused for a moment, wondering if something was wrong.

Turning her head, she focused on him. In the moonlight, he could see the graying at the crown of her head.

Had she been expecting me? Cord shoved the thought away. Of course not. He hadn't even planned to come out here.

Continuing his progression toward her, Genma's bear lifted her snout to the air and dropped it quickly, a greeting. His bear returned the gesture.

Before he could reach her, she turned and trotted back to her house and rounded the porch to her side entrance. He watched Genma shift, wave at him then enter her home. Going around to the front, he started to check the main road leading to her property. He took two steps then stopped instantly. The fur at the back of his neck began to rise. Something or someone was triggering his senses.

Moving slowly he turned his head from left to right, looking closely at every shadow in the woods. Nothing was there that didn't belong. There were a few rabbits out, digging along Genma's garden that he would be re-fertilizing tomorrow. Two owls perched on limbs, but nothing else.

However, the feeling wouldn't go away. If the sensation was not being driven by the forest around him then the only other possibility was the house. *Genma?*

Raising his head, he glanced back at her front door

and the windows of her living room, but he saw nothing. Then he glanced along the side of the house at the other windows. That's when he saw it, a flicker of the curtains at the end room.

Realizing the feeling was coming from within the house, he relaxed. Down the path to the road, he put his snout to the ground and began isolating scents. Pushing aside those of nature and Genma, he focused his search on anything that was familiar, a scent that was out of the ordinary.

~YH~

A bear? Rena's heart stopped beating for a moment as she watched a bear move by the side of her grandmother's house. Just having awakened a few moments ago, she realized that she had slept more hours than she'd anticipated. She glanced out the window as she did most nights at home. More than any other time of the day, she loved the evenings. Moonlit nights drew her.

Not hearing any noise in the house, she was concerned her grandmother may be outside taking in some air and there was a bear around. After releasing the curtain, she rushed down the hall. Her grandmother's bedroom door was still open as it had been earlier, the bed undisturbed. Continuing on, she took in the empty living room.

Turning left, she cleared the threshold of the kitchen and stopped short of plowing down her grandmother who was moving from the kitchen door in a flowing house dress. "Oh, Grandma. I was just checking to see where you were."

"Red, I'm here. How are you feeling?" Going to the sink, her grandmother washed her hands and picked up a kitchen towel to wipe them.

"I'm good. Better than I have been in a while." Not wanting to get distracted with a discussion of her health and forget why she was seeking her grandmother, Rena said, "Were you outside?"

"Yes. Just for a moment. Did you come looking for me? I thought you were still asleep."

"I was. When I looked out the window in my room I saw a bear."

"Hm, did you?" Not seeming at all worried, her grandmother went to the stove and lifted the lid from a medium-size pot. She began to stir the contents with a wooden spoon that had been resting in a dish.

"A big brown bear." Rena leaned against the counter and wondered why her grandmother wasn't more shocked or afraid.

"They are the state animal. I'm sure there are hundreds roaming freely in the forests and mountains of California." Smiling at her, her grandmother went to a cabinet and pulled out two bowls then returned to the stove.

Rena inhaled, calmed herself and let out a breath slowly. "I guess you're right. Living in the city, I can't recall the last time I saw a bear that wasn't in a circus or zoo."

Those words seemed to produce a scowl on her grandmother's face. "Such a shame that animals are held away from their natural habitats to be put on display." Genma shook her head as she ladled in soup for the bowls.

Always having felt the same as her grandmother, Rena remained silent. She was just happy her grandmother was okay. "You know, Grandma, you could move to the city with me."

"Oh, heavens no." The look of horror on her

grandmother's face was almost comical. It was as if Rena had asked her if she wanted to be skinned alive.

Laughing, Rena moved around the lower part of the counter where the stove was to the bar above it and set down the bowls of soup on the marble top. A memory flashed in her mind of her sitting at the bar when she was younger, leaning over to watch her grandmother cook. Her grandmother had just been starting to teach her the skills the last summer Rena was there. Pushing the memory away, she claimed a seat. "This smells wonderful, Grandma."

"I have some rolls from the diner in town." Grabbing a pot holder, Genma stepped to the side of the stove, opened the oven door and pulled out the pan of rolls then turned the dial from warm to off. Moving quickly over to the refrigerator she took out a small plastic container and brought them both to the bar. "You are going to love these. The sweet butter just makes all the difference as well."

"I believe you. At this moment I feel so ravenous, I could eat a bush of blackberries." Rena wasn't joking. Now that the threat of the bear was gone and she'd smelled the soup, her stomach had begun to growl and she was hungry, like she hadn't been since she became ill.

"That is a good sign. Well, bless your food and dig in. There's plenty more if you want it." Slipping onto a high chair, Genma popped open the container and grabbed a roll. Splitting the bread, she slathered a heavy amount of the buttery substance onto it. She set it on a napkin beside Rena's bowl and did the same for herself.

Tasting the first spoonful of soup, Rena moaned. The vegetables in it were chunky but tender, and the broth was savory, creamy and thick. It was the perfect chowder. It was the broth, different from any other she had ever tried before, that seemed to make her want to drink directly from the bowl. Rena was trying to figure out what it consisted of, but the heavy amount of rosemary and fresh parsley was masking it. "Grandma, your cooking is like none other."

"Thank you. But, it's nothing special. This dish is from a friend of mine in town. We all exchange various recipes that we have created during the winter months. That's when most of us have a lot of time on our hands to experiment."

"I can't wait to pick your brain before I leave."

"You could always stay the winter, Red, and I could teach you first hand." Her grandmother continued to eat her own soup, not looking at her.

"Maybe," was her only comment as she continued to eat her soup.

They sat in silence and ate.

After she finished her soup, Rena picked up her roll and bit into it. Just like everything else, the homemade roll and butter were good. "How far is the diner?"

"Town is about ten miles. I'm sure Greta wouldn't mind taking you. You two should get along well." Genma took her bowl to the sink then began pouring the pot of soup into a container.

"I'm sure. However, I really don't want to be a bother to anyone. If you're not taking your car, I could find it myself." Following suit, Rena went to the sink and ran dish water and began collecting utensils and dishes around the kitchen to wash.

"Then I will leave you directions." Genma took the plastic container to the sink.

"Thank you."

In a few minutes, they had the kitchen cleaned and everything put away.

"Well, I'm going to turn in. Octavia and I have an early start in the morning. Can I get you anything before I go?" Her grandmother tossed the paper towel she had been using to wipe her hands into the trash.

"Just tell me where you keep your tea. I want to make another cup of it and maybe do some reading." Rena felt like stripping off her clothes and running in the moonlight more than a cup of tea, but that was insane. So, instead she opted for a good book.

"Excellent. It is in the small canister beside the kettle on the stove." Genma pointed at the blue and white tin. "I believe there is enough for another cup or two. When you need more, it is in the pantry in a tin with the same decoration, just bigger."

"Oh, good. I might go insane if I ran out before you returned." Rena smiled. She picked up the kettle and filled it with water from the faucet.

Laughing, Genma crossed the kitchen to her and kissed her on her cheek. "I can't say enough that I'm glad to have you here, Red."

Hugging her, Rena said, "I'm happy to be here. It was just what I needed."

Genma pulled away. "I will be gone by the time you get up."

"Grandma, you can wake me. I'll help you get your things into Mrs. Octavia's car." Rena set the kettle on the eye and turned on the range to heat the water.

"No, need. You should rest. Use this time to enjoy yourself, eat and regain your strength." Her grandmother started out of the kitchen then stopped. "I need to show you how the radio works so you can contact people, if you need to."

Leaving the kitchen, Rena followed the energetic older woman. Her grandmother crossed the living room to a wooden cabinet that had a Citizens' Band radio. Genma went through instructions of how to use it and select one of forty different channels.

She pulled the drawer beneath it open and showed her the address book with names and two digit numbers. "Here is a list of all of the families in Den County and their channel, the mayor and sheriff's offices included. If you leave and want to take communication with you, this is the handheld."

It was so strange to be in the twenty-first century and be in a community that didn't have telephones and cell phones. It was a different way of life in Den that was for sure.

"Got it. Do you think the sheriff will allow me to use the phone later in the week to call my doctor and let her know how I'm doing?"

"You sure can. Tell the quack your grandmother had the cure." Genma patted Rena's cheek.

Laughing, Rena shook her head at her grandmother's comment. She couldn't discount it since she had felt a hundred times better since getting here hours ago. Rena was sure that if her strength and health continued to improve, she would be back to her old self by the end of the week. Maybe she would be able to get her old job back.

"Well, goodnight, Red."

"Goodnight, Grandma." Rena watched her grandmother strut proudly through the living room until she entered and closed her bedroom door behind her.

Hearing the kettle whistle, Rena went to the kitchen and fixed herself a cup of tea. A few minutes later she was curled up on the corner of the couch with an original copy of Zora Neale Hurston's *Their Eyes Were Watching God*. The cover was laminated, protected and preserved with pages yellowed from time in between.

She'd loved this book for years, and normally had no problem becoming engaged in it once she started, however, she found her gaze frequently being drawn to the patio door. Twice she had been ready to set the book down and go for a walk to the lake, but the thought of the bear, which may still be somewhere around, kept her rooted to her seat.

The last thing she wanted was a face-to-face with something big and furry, imposing. Allowing her mind to drift to the large animal for a moment, she recalled how its brown hair had seemed to shimmer in the moonlight. Its movements were fluid for such a huge beast as he walked toward her grandmother's driveway.

She'd never thought about bears being beautiful, and as massive as the one she'd seen had been it seemed like the word didn't truly describe it well. Stunning and arresting probably was better. Even now she wished bears were more friendly creatures because she would love to rub her hands along the powerful muscles of its back and feel if the fur was soft or coarse.

"Let it go, Rena." *My name wasn't Grizzly James Adams and that wasn't Ben.*

Hopefully the bear would be far away by morning and stay away the rest of the week.

~YH~

A while later Cord still found himself circling Genma's property. He'd circled twice, unsure why he had not headed home yet. Something was gnawing deep in his gut, but he wasn't sure what. There was nothing amiss at Genma's. He sensed the hour was getting late and he had work to do come morning. Shaking off the impression, he moved back toward the path to the lake giving the area one last sniff and that's when he smelled it.

Mine. His bear claimed.

He followed the scent from a tree to the docks. It was different than Genma's markings. This scent reminded him of honeyed asters: floral, sweet and intoxicating. Something seemed familiar about it, but he couldn't place any female in the county he'd recalled having such an aroma. Even though the flower grew wild around the county, he knew it wasn't the same as the plant. It was similar, but more original, and different.

Maybe someone had visited Genma recently, an unmated female from town that had possibly just come into maturity. It was possible that in his effort to avoid taking just any female Were, he was grasping at straws.

Part of him believed that he was making up the smell. That he'd become so overwhelmed by the pressures on him to find a life mate, it was possible he was conjuring up some illusive Were-female.

However, the other part of him, his bear, whined and pawed the ground. It wanted to stay there in the woods until it could locate the female. That wasn't going to happen. Tomorrow was soon enough.

Giving his bear a mental nudge until he began to meander back toward the miles leading home, Cord allowed one final glance toward the dock, then carried on.

He had every intention of rising early to attempt to catch Genma before she left with his grandmother and question the woman about visitors she'd had in the last few days.

CHAPTER FIVE

She was hidden to him. His bear stood at the beginning of the dock, staring at her silhouette at the end. The moon hovered behind the night clouds, refusing to come out to illuminate the female before him.

Even though he couldn't see her, he could smell her. Her scent seemed to be all around him, powerful. It had obliterated everything else around him and had him isolating on nothing but her aroma. Unable to resist he moved his front paw, stepping on the wooden planks. Each of his steps was accompanied by a deep inhale. He couldn't get enough of the aphrodisiac of her skin.

Mid-step he shifted, never halting in his approach.

When he finally stopped, he stood before her, feeling the heat of her skin. So close, yet he still he couldn't make out her features. The fact that he had found her would not allow him to be disappointed that he couldn't identify her. Closing his eyes, he allowed his sense of smell to acquaint himself with her.

"Cord..." she whispered his name. Her voice, sultry, stroked his core.

He wanted to demand she touch him, but his throat was too tight, his bear still too close to the surface. It was always like that during mating time. It was the only moment where both man and bear were operating as one. Both played a significant role even though the male form was present, dominant.

Growling low, Cord leaned in, setting his nose along her neck. Taking a deep breath, he drew in honeyed asters. It was like oxygen to his soul.

Touching her with nothing but his nose, he lowered his body and moved past her collarbone to the skin between her breasts.

She was trembling and her heart was pounding. A bawdy symphony accompanied by the hard, heavy rhythm of his own. He felt calm, steady, even though there were emotions and desires rocketing through his body and demanding more. Demanding he claim her in the oldest way and make her his before she escaped him.

Not giving in to the demands of his body, he had to continue on. Find the central point where her nectar was strongest. He traveled past the supple skin of her stomach but as he attempted to locate what he craved the most, it eluded him.

Instead of her scent becoming stronger it grew fainter. *No.*

Trying to capture more of her smell, the main identity of a bear's mate, he inhaled deeper. Yet, he could not fill his lungs with it, with her.

The darkness seemed to swallow her up. Drag her away from him. Dropping to his knees, he reached out in an attempted to grasp the willowy form. Nothing.

Frustrated, he opened his eyes. She was gone. The moon now illuminated the lake, the forest and the empty dock before him.

Rrrraaaahhhhhhaaaa!

The agonized growl of his bear shattered the night image before him, quaked his soul and awakened him.

Startled, Cord sat up, blinking against the rising brightness of the morning sun. Looking from left to right, he was shocked to see he was in bed at home, not on the dock.

It had all been a dream. She had been a dream

"Shit!" Falling back against the bed, he ran his hand over his face. Everything had seemed so real, compelling. He knew what had caused the vision in his mind, the trace of a faint scent at Genma's.

Tipping his head back on the pillow, he stared upwards at the painting Genma had given him — a lake with an empty dock.

"Genma." *Damn it.* Shoving off the cover, he launched from the bed. He'd wanted to be at her house before dawn to try and see her before she left with his grandmother. Now he was running late. The sun's position, barely above the trees, let him know it was almost eight in the morning. In the fall, it rose later than the summer months.

He was angry with his bear for being so fixated on the damn scent it had conjured up a fantasy that Cord couldn't release himself from until it was over. He rushed into the bathroom in his bedroom and washed his face and brushed his teeth, thankful that he'd had the foresight to shower last night after he returned.

In his bedroom, he went to the dresser and pulled out jeans and a t-shirt then got a pair of clean socks.

Minutes later, he padded out of his bedroom directly into the sitting room, the only other room on the second floor of his house. Reaching the CB radio stand at the far end of the couch, he dialed the channel to his grandparents' station.

"Morning, Cord." His grandfather, Benat Bjorn, answered his call sign. "Is everything okay?"

Depressing the button, Cord responded, "Hi, PawPaw. Everything is just fine. I was trying to reach Nana. Is she in?"

"Nope. You know her and Genma were out before dawn even crested, like they were being run out of town." His grandfather chuckled, no concern in his voice.

He knew it was a long shot to hope his grandmother was still in town, but he knew his bear would give him no peace if he didn't at least try. Groaning, Cord ran his hand over his head.

"You still there, son?" A small note of worry came through the line.

It amazed Cord how his grandfather could be perfectly fine with his wife and her friend going out on some Thelma and Louise adventure during the First Frost Moon Festival, but become vexed from a moment of silence from his grandson. Just proved to Cord that all of his family was troubled by his lack of a life mate.

Did they see me as weak? A defective bear that was going to be the leader of their community?

Squeezing his free hand into a fist, Cord fought against the budding rage.

Holding down the button, Cord wanted to set the older man at ease. "I'm here. Things are fine."

"Anything I can help you with in your nana's absence?"

"No, PawPaw. Really I was trying to ask a couple questions of Genma before they left." Cord rubbed his chin, hearing the scratch of the stubble there. In his rush, he hadn't shaved this morning. Soon he'd have to be more meticulous about his image. As mayor over Den County, he would be the face of the community. Even his long hair would have to go.

"Ah. That's right, your grandmother mentioned you would be taking care of something for her friend. Well, I'm sure you'll sort it all out." Confidence in Cord's ground maintenance skills was evident in his grandfather's light tone.

"Thanks. Well, gotta go."

"I understand, you have work to do and all."

Soon they ended the connection with sincere vows of love and respect. Not wanting to waste any more time on his day, Cord moved downstairs to the first floor where his living room, kitchen and two guest rooms were located. After a quick breakfast of honeyed sausages between whole grain bread and a cup of coffee, he stepped into his work boots at the door leading into his garage.

Ten minutes later, he was on his way to his shop in town for the additional supplies he would need for Genma's yard. He could take one of his assistants, but this was something he needed to do alone. He would stretch out the job for the week and keep him away from town.

Burying his hands deep in dirt and soil was just what he needed to shove all the anger, worry and issues plaguing him to the back of his mind.

~YH~

Her growling stomach woke her the next morning. She'd slept more peacefully than she ever did at home in her own bed. Before coming here, she would have thought that sleeping without all the city sounds would have been difficult for her, but the soft bird calls outside the window were soothing. Reaching over to the nightstand, she grabbed her cell phone beside the book she had been reading the night before. Her phone was something she used more for time than anything else. There was absolutely no cell connection in Den County, she had checked. Seeing that it was almost ten in the morning, she didn't even try to fool herself to thinking her grandmother was still around.

If she hadn't come to Den to rest and recuperate, she would have been appalled she'd slept so late. She'd always been an early riser, up with the sun. Slipping from her cocoon, she stood beside the bed. She waited for the wave of nausea that always greeted her in the mornings when she rose. Feeling nothing, she let out a sigh and went into the bathroom.

After a quick shower, she pulled on her robe and went to find sustenance. She had a craving for her grandmother's muffins. As soon as she entered the kitchen, she grabbed one from the tin and devoured it while she stood in front of the open refrigerator deciding what else to cook.

Licking the sticky sweetness from her fingers, she decided on cream of wheat and eggs. Not as devout a vegan as her mother, Rena enjoyed an egg and other dairy products every now and then. Instead of grabbing the stick of butter to fry her eggs in, she opted for the sweet butter her grandmother said was from the diner in town.

She was thankful that she was feeling better, because consuming so many sweets was going to swell her hips, more than they already were, and she would need to exercise.

Once her breakfast was made, she set the plate on the bar. The only thing missing was a sweetener for her cream of wheat. She went to the pantry for the agave nectar her grandmother had picked up for her.

At the door down the short hall from the back door, she flicked the light switch then opened the pantry. Entering the small room, she was amazed to see the many shelves of homemade canned fruits and vegetables as well as other staple items. Her grandmother had enough stuff in there to hold her over for several months.

Spotting what she was looking for, she stepped into the room and grabbed the bottle on the shelf in front of her. Turning to leave, she halted in her steps. Before her eyes, on the shelves adjacent to the door, had to be more than a hundred jars of honey.

Since she had arrived at her grandmother's house and begun to feel better, she had not thought about the cravings that had plagued her. Now, having one of them less than an arm reach away, the desire for the golden syrup crashed into her like a tidal wave.

The salivation started first, followed by the tremors in her limbs that ended with heat. Her temperature spiked so high she was sweating. Not just a light sheen of sweat, but her palms were damp, a bead of perspiration was running under one breast and her bare thighs beneath her terry cloth robe were slick.

One taste. A voice called out from inside of her, seeming both a part of her and separate at the same time.

"I shouldn't." Rena argued, feeling as if she were losing her mind. Lifting a hand, she caressed the cool glass trapping the honey from her fingers.

One taste.

I have to get out of here. Rena felt as if her feet were rooted to the floor as she fought against her indecision.

~YH~

It wasn't the smell of fried eggs, or the warm fragrant scent of steamed wheat that bombarded his senses when he entered Genma's home. After spending the last two hours pulling up the summer flowers and preparing the soil for the winter buds he would plant, he'd come inside for the instructions Genma said she would leave for him.

He had not gotten more than two steps past the back door before he picked up on it, honeyed asters. Stronger than the light trace he'd detected last night by the lake, it was now heavy and saturating the air.

His bear, who was normally subdued during the day, reared up inside of him and propelled Cord to action.

Hunt. Claim.

Cord's vision became narrowed. Everything around him was painted in a golden hue. His body became tight, as each hair on his arms and the back of his neck rose. Need burned through his body, setting his blood on fire.

Moving on nothing but animal instinct to locate the source of the scent, he turned right down the short hall. The only thing before him was the door leading to Genma's pantry. However, before he could enter it, he was struck hard by something against his chest.

Not something, but someone. Her.

He didn't even have time to make out her blurred form as she'd come running out of the pantry as if she was being stalked by something. Then she was in his arms.

His mind shut off and his body responded. No time to weigh the right and wrong of it, he pulled her to him and lowered his mouth to hers.

Cupping her face, he held her against him. Not giving her any space to deny him what he wanted. Her. Not a request. No permission. Like some Roman gladiator, he was willing to conquer anything that stood in the way of his kissing her. His woman.

His bear knew it from a whiff of her scent.

Cord knew it from the moment he tasted her.

If she would have fought against him, he would not have been shocked. However, she didn't. She gave back to him all the fierce passion that he showed her.

They bumped up against something. He wasn't even aware he'd moved forward. Pressing closer, he sandwiched her between himself and the structure. The taste of her mouth was sweet and hot, like warm honey. He couldn't get enough.

She buried her hands in his hair, pulling the cool strands out of the band that held it back while he worked. He didn't care. He wanted to make a mess of her as well.

He had to assure himself that she wasn't a mirage. That he wasn't dreaming and she wasn't a figment of his imagination, again. His mouth left hers and trailed down her chin, tasting her scent. The savory flavor of her skin and the smell of her heat was a cornucopia of pleasures to his senses.

She sighed.

Pulling open her robe, he touched her. The delicate curve of her waist was softer than silk against his fingertips. She was real.

His cock was hard, swollen with the demand to be sheathed inside of her and to claim her, marking her as his forever. His bear rejoiced, and a low growl broke forth from his lips as he licked the upper swell of her breast.

She placed her hand against his chest, her fingers flexed and dug into his pec.

"I need you... Let me in. Don't deny us." Snatching her robe wider and off her shoulder, he glided his tongue lower ready to suckle the tight twin peaks.

"What was—wait—stop!" She shoved him.

He felt the stinging slap on his cheek. The impact barely turned his head. His mind was a fog of lust, but her resistance and assault was a wind of sanity clearing the haze. Dropping his hands from her, he stepped back. He didn't want to, and every foot of space that he created between the two of them was painful, a stab in the gut.

Bumping against the wall a short distance across from the pantry, he dragged in several breaths, filling his lungs. The madness of lust was slow to clear as he took in the beautiful black female before him. Slender with sienna-kissed skin, the color of Native American clay. She had a narrow waist but hips so full he could imagine holding them firmly as he pounded his cock deep inside of her. His dick twitched in approval.

Noticing his gaze along her body, the female before him yanked the sides of her robe together, shutting him off from the tantalizing view. He clenched his fist to keep from reaching out and ripping the robe away from her body and shredding it.

"Who are you?" There was a tremor to her voice, but it still maintained a sultry huskiness.

Her words pulled his gaze to her face and he was struck by a bolt of lightning. She had the face of one of the Great Spirit's angels. He took in the oval shape, with her broad nose, wide lips so plump he could kiss them for hours. Her eyes were hazel with a hint of gold sparkling in their depth. A Were-bear, but not.

"Did you hear me? Explain yourself. What kind of person comes into someone's house and accosts them? Not a sane one that's for sure." She folded her arms over her breasts and eyed him.

It was her unique hazel eyes that clued him in to who she was, after all these years. "It's you."

She frowned. "What? Of course I'm me. The question was, who the *hell* are you?"

"You don't remember? Remember me?" He banged his head back against the wooden wall.

Staring at him, she allowed her gaze to travel along his body from head to toe. Her perusal was causing the heat that had lowered to a simmer to spike again.

He stifled a growl.

Evidently, not enough, he thought as he watched her head lift sharply.

Tilting her head, she looked into his face. "What's wrong with your eyes?" She sounded breathless, as she said, "They're gold."

Better to see your lust with, my dear.

He pushed the bold words away and considered the female before him. Not as unaffected by him as she was trying to make him believe. However, he hadn't been convinced anyway, not only from the passion in her kiss earlier, but by the scent of her arousal that was still teasing him from the three-foot distance.

Lowering his head, he closed his eyes and took a deep breath. He inhaled two more times, trying to think calming thoughts instead of the female before him. Once he felt a little more at ease and less like he wanted to pounce across the floor at her, he opened his eyes.

When the pucker in her brows deepened, showing confusion in her features, it was a declaration that his eyes had returned to black. Instead of answering her last question, he said, "I'm Cord. Cord Bjorn, Rena."

The lids around her hazel eyes stretched wide with shock. "How do you know my name? Did my grandmother tell you I was here?"

"I have never forgotten a thing about the last time I saw you. Or you." He confessed. It was the truth. Over the years his memory of her had begun to fade, but not how he felt about her. Not about the experience of the first time his eyes had shifted to gold. It had been when he kissed her.

They had been so young then. She had blossomed from the girl she was into a real beauty.

"You don't recall."

Pushing off the wall, she moved into the kitchen. Standing by the sink she kept her back to him. "I'd only come for a week or two in the summer and it's been too many years since the last time I was here. How could I remember?"

Hearing those words was like a weight crushing on his heart. However, he wouldn't give up, not this time. She was his.

Now that the heat had cleared his mind, some, he was able to have more lucid thoughts. Something was wrong. As a Were-female she should not have been able to resist the mating lust once it was upon them. Her return kiss had been passionate, desperate and fierce, yet still restrained.

Inhaling deeply, wanting to capture her scent, imprint it on his soul, he became more aware of the problem. Under the floral honey notes of her scent, there should have been marking of her species—Werebear markings. Rena's was faint. Almost as if she was a young Were. One just coming into maturity.

However, she had to be close to thirty and that change took place around their sixteenth human year. Like how old he was the first time he'd kissed her.

"Why have you stayed away so long?"

She glanced at him over her shoulder then turned to face him, slowly. "I don't know what business that is of yours. I'm still trying to figure out how I can get you out of this house and off my grandmother's property."

A single corner of his mouth kicked up, she was a bold saucy thing. He liked his women with backbone. "You can't. I'm here to do a job for Genma while she's gone."

She lowered her head, dropping it into her hands. "Oh, goodness, that's right...the landscaper was coming."

"In the flesh." Widening his stance, he folded his arms over his chest.

Raising her head, she gave him a small smile. A false smile that didn't reach her eyes. "Look, you're here to do a job. So, we will just keep out of each other's way and chalk up the kiss to a mistake."

"It wasn't," he declared.

The smile slipped some. "Okay, we will say...you were expecting someone else."

"I wasn't."

The smile on her mouth was only held in place because she was clenching her teeth. "Would you prefer that I radio the sheriff and tell him you accosted me?"

Laughter rumbled through his chest and exploded into the room as he tipped his head back letting it free.

"I'm not sure what you see is so funny."

She would if she were fully Were. Sheriff Smokey would walk into the house and take one whiff of the heat boiling between them and Cord's golden gaze and know what was going on. The law man would turn right around and leave. In Den County the law didn't interfere in life mate issues. The mates were expected to work it out or die trying.

Composing himself, he said, "It would take too long to explain and as you said, I have work to do."

"Well, then you should get to it." Grabbing both ends of her belt, she pulled it tighter then moved to the bar. "Now, you have already made my breakfast cold, so if you will excuse me."

"How about I cook dinner for you tonight?" He moved closer to her and noticed the pulse in her neck leap at his nearness. Definitely not unaffected like she wanted him to believe.

It was her turn to laugh. "You've got to be kidding me. After the kiss in the pantry, I'd be crazy to think I'd be safe at a strange man's home."

Lifting his hand, he caressed the side of her face with a finger, sweeping it down under her plump bottom lip. He felt the quake that rocketed through his body as the small contact caused a shudder in her body, but thankfully she didn't draw away from him or slap him again.

"You will always be safe with me, my hazel-eyed beauty. I will give my life to protect you."

There was a small intake of breath as she stared at him with her innocent gaze.

Moving away, he headed into the living room. Spotting the list on the end table, he grabbed it then exited the house by the patio door. His mate needed time. Time to *accept* what was happening between them. Time to see what was *going* to happen.

He needed to sort out what was going on with her and her bear. More than he did this morning, he wished he had caught Genma and his grandmother before they had left. He had so many questions. Things it didn't seem that Rena could answer.

But no matter what he discovered, one day soon the moment would be right for him to claim her.

Mine, his bear growled as Cord closed the door.

"Yes, she is."

~YH~

Rena put her cold breakfast into the microwave. Right now her throat was so tight with emotions and her mind was twisted with so many thoughts and questions that she couldn't eat. Cord Bjorn had walked into the cabin and turned her world upside down.

She wasn't a novice to lust or sex. Over the years she'd had boyfriends. Hell, just eight months ago she would have been willing to settle for a guy she liked well enough, had even thought maybe he was the one. However, he broke it off with her once she started getting sick and could barely drag herself out of bed. Then she'd seen clearly that he was not the man for her.

But none of those past men had prepared her for Cord. An intense male, so devastating in presence and body that she felt restricted on all sides. She'd never encountered a man so...big. That was the only word that came to her mind. He wasn't only a tall man–he had to be close to six eight—but the width of his shoulders was massive. He had the height of a basketball player with the girth of a linebacker and just as many rippling muscles. However, the way his shirt and jeans conformed to the contours of all those bulging muscles she didn't see an ounce of fat. Thank goodness her grandmother's doors were wider than normal, because Rena was sure he would not have been able to fit through them without turning sideways. Shockingly, his large size didn't cause fear to race through her blood. Actually quite the opposite. His overwhelming presence made her feel feminine and protected.

I'd love to have him at my back...or front...or underneath – She put a halt to the wayward thoughts tripping around in her head.

Unable to stop herself from thinking of the tall, bulky frame again caused shivers of heat to run rampant in her body. Her nipples were still tight and her sex was throbbing, all from a kiss. No matter what she had said to him, she had no apprehension, but something else. Lust and overpowering desire to tear his clothing off and have his massive body thrusting deep inside of her.

Oh, damn...

Seeing something move beyond the window, she stepped to it and stared out taking in the man. He was busy digging into the earth, almost wrist deep as he set bulbs and plants into holes he created with his hands. Those hands had been all over her, caressing her.

Just like the rest of him, they were big—wide strong hands—that knew how to touch a woman. The white v-neck t-shirt he wore clung to the landscape of his torso. Those broad shoulders would provide a place for a woman's legs to rest as he pounded into her sex.

Your legs. She ignored the low voice inside of her, proof that she was truly losing her mind.

The fact that she was standing at her grandmother's

kitchen window admiring the landscaper was just more verification.

However, she couldn't pull her gaze away. When he had been in the house, she could have sworn she could count the ridges of the six-pack on his abs. Now, as he squatted in the dirt she could see how the black jeans he wore hugged his thighs and ass. Only her mind flashed a picture of him leaning against the wall by the pantry and how the denim had cupped his cock.

I shouldn't have looked. But, she could not stop herself then just like she was unable to resist the view of him now.

More than his body and what her thoughts told her he could do to her with it, it was his face. A kind face with dark eyes so astounding that they seemed to see into her heart, mark her soul. The two-day stubble that covered the lower half of his face and the long wheat-blonde hair that she had fisted in her hands made his look. A wild man that could not be tamed.

Evident in the kiss he had given her, it had been unleashed and demanding.

As if feeling her gaze, he looked up and stared directly into the window. Gasping, she quickly stepped to the side hoping that the bright light of the sun outside had hindered him from seeing her inside.

Damn it.

Peeping back out, she saw that he was not only still looking toward her, but smiling as well. When he winked, she turned and rushed to her room.

In the room, she stood before the mirror over the dresser and observed the woman staring back at her. The same woman who had come to the woods in hopes of restoring her health, instead she had stumbled into the arms of a man who in one kiss had showed her a passion like she'd never known.

How could she feel so different inside since the last twenty-four hours, but still be the same on the outside.

What she really expected to see was evidence of the lie she had told Cord. She had said she didn't recall her time in Den County when she was younger. Had alleged that she didn't recall him. Everything else may be fuzz in her head, trapped in storage her mother had created, but when Cord had kissed her everything about him had been revealed in bold, brassy color.

Both the minty, heady taste of him and the gold tone of his gaze had bared the memory to her. Even standing there in the room she could see the two of them sitting on the dock, him teaching her how to fish and then the kiss. Even at thirteen she had noted the small ripples of desire she felt being around Cord. Their kiss had been brief but earth shifting, until her mother had screamed her name as if she'd committed a cardinal sin.

When her mother dragged her away from him, Rena had glanced back and was captured in his confused golden gaze. She didn't understand the meaning or the reason for his eye color change, then or now, but she knew she needed to keep far away from the intense man.

"You just have to make it through the week, Rena. Then once your grandmother comes home you can be on the first plane speeding out of California."

CHAPTER SIX

"Well, look who finally remembered where they live." Changing from animal to human, Cord called out to the big brown bear coming down the path toward him.

The other bear shifted and became a man just as big as Cord. "Kiss my ass." Theo laughed at Cord's ribbing. "One sec and I'll get you a pair of pants to put on so you can come in for coffee and biscotti."

"I see how it is, you don't want to tempt your wife with a more virile Were-male." Cord followed his good friend to the Kodiak family cabin.

"Keep dreaming." Theo entered his house by the laundry room then tossed out a pair of jeans to Cord.

After he got the pants on and fastened, Cord took the steps two at a time.

"Well, hello, Cord." Riley, Theo's life mate of a year, moved from her husband's arms and crossed the kitchen to Cord.

He gave her a fierce hug and received the same in

return. "It's good to see you, Riley. How are your parents?"

"Wonderful." She stepped back and smiled. "They could not get enough of the boys and their newest granddaughter."

"I bet." He took one of two mugs of coffee Theo was carrying. "Where are the little ones now?" Except for their conversation, Cord noticed the house was quiet.

"Thankfully, they are sleeping. They were out before we crossed into Den." Theo sat at the head of the long wooden table.

Cord claimed a side seat and reached for the jar in the center of the table, an abundant staple in all Den residents cabin home. Adding a large dollop of honey into his coffee he then pushed it toward Theo.

"Well, I will leave you bear males to yourselves." Riley placed a plate of her homemade mixed-berry biscotti on the table between them.

"You're leaving and sticking me with this guy's company?" Cord aimed a finger at Theo.

Laughing, Riley walked to her mate and kissed him. Cord noticed that Theo didn't want to be out of his wife's presence, by the thick arm surrounding her waist.

"I'll make him promise to be on his best behavior. Or he won't get any more treats tonight." She wiggled out of her husband's arm then blew him a kiss and headed out.

"No fair. I don't even like this guy. Now, how I treat him is weighed against my life mate privileges." Theo growled.

Riley just shook her head at both of them and left the kitchen.

Cord chuckled.

After his wife was completely out of sight, Theo grabbed a biscotti stick and said, "Thanks for keeping an eye on our place while we were gone last week."

"Hey, it's nothing. You did the same for me when I left last year."

"I was glad when you told me you didn't have plans to vacate the county this year." Theo dipped his stick several times into his coffee before biting into it. "So, have you decided to claim an available female this year and take your rightful place over the residents?"

As he took a big bite of his dry stick, Cord thought about his friend's question, and allowed his mind to drift back to this time yesterday. So much had changed. Rena had come back into his life.

"Well, you look like the bear who found an empty hive of honey."

Unable to hold back the smile that pulled at the corners of his mouth, Cord looked up at his friend. "Do I?"

"Hell, yeah. What's up?" Theo lifted his mug and drank.

"I plan to claim my life mate."

Frowning, Theo lowered his coffee back to the table. "Well, you've always told me that you don't believe Marcella is your mate, have you changed your mind?"

Cord took a healthy swig of his coffee. "No. Not at all."

"Damn it, don't keep me in suspense, bear, who is it? And what the hell happened in the week I've been gone?"

"My mate showed up."

"Showed up? A new family come to Den or something?" Theo leaned back in the chair and stared at him.

Slowly shaking his head, Cord considered dragging it out or leaving and making his friend wait until Theo found out himself. However, Theo was too good of a friend for him to do it. Not to mention Cord needed someone to talk to about it.

"Do you remember Genma's granddaughter, Rena?" Cord took another bite of his stick.

Staring off into the distance, Theo's features scrunched as if he were attempting to dig into an old memory.

"Genma's daughter Lillian had a little girl that would come up during the summer when we were younger, right?"

"Yes." Cord confirmed.

"So, what does that have to do with you? The daughter nor the granddaughter have been seen in Den for maybe fifteen years."

"Well, Rena is back, now."

Lifting, both eyebrows, Theo stared at him. "Really? Why after all this time?"

Cord shrugged. "There's a lot I don't know. But, I'm sure Genma has most of the answers, but she went with my nana on some secret trip."

"Well, that's damn convenient."

"Hell, yeah, it is. So, Rena is staying at Genma's and I'm contracted to do some work out there this week." Cord ran his hand over his head, frustrated. "You could have dragged me out to the lake and drowned me and I would not have been more shocked then when I walked into Genma's house and was doused by Rena's scent." Remembering the impact of her intoxicating scent on him and his response to it, Cord's hands began to shake. Even now he wanted her. He balled them into tight fists. There was no way he could allow himself to go to her tonight. He'd already *assaulted* Rena once today. The next time he touched her, he knew his bear would not let him stop until he had marked her.

Theo nodded slowly. "Ah, I see. Trust me, if anyone knows what it is like to have an unexpected encounter with not only an available Were-female, but one's life mate, I do."

Cord and Theo had gone out for a run one night months ago and Theo had filled him in on what had happened between him and Riley when she'd crashed her car down the road from Theo's cabin. They had discovered that they'd met previously and Theo had unknowingly marked her, causing Riley to carry Were-bear markings in her scent. "Well, my situation is not so different from yours."

"How? Did you bite her one of those summers she was coming up here?"

He wished. Then maybe things would be a little easier. "No. I kissed her once then. Hell, that may have been the catalyst that made her mother keep her way. Who knows."

Theo dunked the other half of his biscotti. "That's doubtful. You couldn't have been but maybe sixteen at the time. You would have posed no threat."

Staring down into the remainder of his coffee, Cord considered whether or not to go into details with Theo about the full incident.

His silence must have been telling, because Theo said, "What is it?"

Raising his gaze, Cord confessed, "My first golden haze happened."

"No shit?"

"No shit. It did it again today when I kissed her," he

explained.

"Well, I'll be damned." Theo chuckled. "Do you plan to claim her before or during the Bear Run?"

Shoving his lose hair back from his face in frustration, Cord exhaled hard. "It's complicated."

Theo rose and walked to the counter and poured himself another cup of coffee. "Because she's Genma's granddaughter?"

Cord rose as well, but instead of going for a refill he placed his mug in the sink. "No, because something is off with Rena."

"I'm not following."

Leaning back against the sink, Cord said, "I can't explain it. It's like she doesn't know she's Were."

"How's that possible? She's Genma's kin and she'd spent vacations in Den. Granted she was young, but how can she not know?"

"I don't know. I've been racking my brain all day trying to figure it out. When my eyes turned this morning she didn't know why it happened."

"She didn't recognize that it was brought on by your desire for her?" Still holding his mug high, Theo folded his arms across his chest.

"Exactly." Shaking his head, Cord pushed away from the sink. "Look, you have a mate awaiting you. I'm going to head home."

Theo patted him on the shoulder. "Trust me. One way or another it will work itself out."

Cord headed to the door. "I hope so." Opening the side door, he exited the house and shut the door behind him. At the bottom of the stairs he started to unfasten the jeans Theo had loaned him, when he heard his name.

Turning, Cord faced Theo who was standing on the

top step.

"Let me guess, you need pointers on what to do with that pretty life mate of yours in bed."

"Not from your cocky ass I don't. Hell, compared to me, you are well out of practice."

"If that ain't the fucking truth." Cord agreed. "What's up?"

Moving one step down, Theo said, "I'm not sure if this means anything, but if I'm not mistaken when Lillian left Den when she was younger, I recall there were whispers about her marrying a human, non-shifter."

"So did you." Cord wasn't understanding where his friend was going with this information.

"Yes, but Riley became a Were. I don't think Lillian's husband was ever changed. At least he's never come to Den to prove the rumors wrong."

"Thanks, Theo. I think you may have hit on something."

"I hope it helps." Theo told him.

Stripping out of the jeans, Cord tossed them at Theo then said, "So do I." In a flash, Cord shifted and his bear was off.

"Ass." Theo called out to him, his voice filled with gaiety.

Cord was glad he had done the final check at Theo's place even though his friend had told him he'd be back by Monday. It had given Cord the opportunity to get some of his worries off his mind. Even though being around Theo had stirred up more questions, Cord at least felt like he was moving toward a path that would lead to a future with his life mate.

Now how he was going to get Rena to drop her guard and let her bear out, he didn't know.

~YH~

Hearing the knock at the door, Rena tossed out a quick prayer that it wasn't Cord. All day long she had been on pins and needles, knowing he was once again outside the cabin working in the yard. She had kept herself away from the windows, refusing to let him catch her staring at him again. As if it wasn't bad enough that this man had haunted her dreams, this morning she had awakened with her thighs coated with her own cream. Ever since that kiss yesterday she'd been in a state of need.

She'd thought about going into town, just to get away from the house and the man, but she didn't want to risk going outside and running into him. Especially with the memory of the powerful kiss they had shared plaguing her.

That low voice in her gut seemed to be pushing her toward going out and taking matters into her own hands, kissing Cord. *Claiming* Cord had been the exact words. However, she'd held herself back. It had been a draining feat but one she'd managed to prevail in so far.

By the second knock, Rena finally decided to answer the door. She wasn't a chicken, she had turned down plenty of men in clubs and at her old job, one wilderness male she could handle. Maybe.

Opening the door, she was relieved to see a statuesque black woman, around her age, on the porch.

"Rena, right?" the woman asked, a wide smile on her mouth.

"Yes. And you are?"

Sticking her hand out, the woman said, "I'm Greta. My parents and I live next door."

"It's nice to meet you, Greta." Rena shook the hand

offered. "Please come in."

Greta crossed the threshold. "Genma asked me to pick up some muffins she'd set aside for the festival."

"I'll get them. I believe my grandmother said they were supposed to go to a woman named Lola Shardik." Rena walked toward the kitchen.

"Correct. I'm headed to town now." Greta called after her.

In the pantry, Rena told herself not to even look at the honey. Just grab the muffins and go. Picking up the large container marked Festival, her eyes caught the sight of a smaller container beside it with CORD written on it. Rena closed her eyes and inhaled. Holding a breath, she tried to keep herself calm. The right thing for her to do was to take the package to Cord, her grandmother had evidently meant for him to have it.

Ignoring it for now, she turned to leave the small room. She stared at the words labeling the batch for sale and refused to allow her gaze to stray.

"Here they are." Rena sighed with relief as she moved back into the living room where Greta was still standing.

"Thanks." Greta took the container. "I can't wait to purchase some of these."

"They are delicious." Rena pulled the front door open, smiling at the thought of how many of her own muffins she had consumed in the last two days. If she kept it up, she would have to start walking laps around the house to keep her weight down. Thank goodness she had plenty of room to spare with all of the pounds she had lost over the year while she'd been ill.

Greta walked past her. "It is the honey. It makes everything better."

"What did you say?" Rena didn't believe she'd heard the other woman correctly.

Turning on the porch, Greta faced her. "It's the honey-glaze that makes the muffins delicious. Everything delicious."

Rena frowned. "That can't be right. I'm allergic. My grandmother knows that."

A similar frown came on Greta's features, brow tight. "What's your allergy to?"

"Honey." Rena said plainly.

Tilting her head, Greta stared at her as if Rena had just popped out a third eye on her nose. "I've never heard of that before. Especially not in Den."

"Well, I'm not from Den. So, evidently my grandmother must have made my batch with agave nectar."

"Do you happen to have any of your batch left?"

Laughing, Rena said, "Barely. I've been consuming them almost on the hour." Turning she went into the kitchen and located her tin. Opening it, she took out one of the three muffins remaining then got a butter knife to cut it in half. Once that was done she went back to the door and handed it to the other woman.

Greta didn't waste any time before sinking her teeth into the treat. Chewing slowly, she moaned. "Oh, goodness, they are so good," she mumbled around the mouthful.

"Agave, right?"

"Absolutely not, pure raw honey." Greta popped the other half into her mouth and smiled around it, her dark eyes shining bright with joy.

Rena was floored. All her life, her mother and physicians had said she had a honey allergy. Her mother had cautioned her with a horrible story about when Rena had eaten honey when she was too young to remember, saying she'd almost died. Broken out in hives and fever. Now to find out, that not only did she not have an allergy to the sappy sweetness, but she craved it. *Did my mother lie to me? For what purpose would she have told such a tale?*

"Maybe you grew out of it." Greta declared, now having completely consumed the muffin.

"You're probably right." Absently, Rena nodded, still trying to make heads or tails of it all.

"Well, I'm off to town." Headed to the steps, Greta stopped and faced her again. "You want to come. Get out the house?"

"Um. I was considering it, but I don't kno—"

"Hey, Greta!"

Just the sound of the deep masculine voice and its husky rumble caused heat to spread out from her core into the rest of her body. *How could someone's voice make me feel so needy?*

Turning to the side, Greta's ready smile appeared on her face, almost too wide for Rena.

"Hello to you, Cord. I see you're working hard over here. You're going to miss the festival events if you keep this up."

"I'll catch some things sooner or later." He responded.

Rena leaned against the doorjamb and kept her gaze fixed toward the trees in front of her grandmother's house, denying herself a glance at Cord. He was already haunting her mind when she was asleep and awake. She was too afraid what would come next if she gave herself leave.

"Well, there's going to be a dance tomorrow night, this year. You'll get a chance to show all the females in town your moves." Greta called out laughing.

A sound filled the air, like an animal's growl.

Greta looked at her and laughed. "Down girl, Cord and I are only friends. If you want to claim him, you'll get no blocking from me."

Shocked, Rena slapped her palm over her mouth. She couldn't believe that sound had come from her lips. She didn't know what had come over her. Lowering her hand, she said, "Oh, goodness... what? No, it's nothing like that for him. I mean me... us."

"Which ever. You want to come with me?"

Rena looked at the sexy, beast of a man leaning on his hoe casually. However, the intense look he was giving her was anything but casual.

Mine.

Blocking out the "Sybil-ish" voice inside her, Rena quickly agreed. "I'm going with you. One second."

"I'll be in my truck." Greta moved down the steps.

Rena rushed back into the house and went to her room to get a light jacket. Then went to the kitchen and in there she entered the panty and grabbed the container marked for Cord. Going out of the house, she headed to the silver truck parked behind Cord's black one.

Passing his truck, Rena set the muffins on the hood of it then continued past to the passenger side door of Greta's truck.

She was grateful that Greta did not ask about the tin now resting on Cord's vehicle. When Greta backed out, Rena allowed herself a quick glance at Cord. Her breath became seized in her chest when she saw that he had not moved, but he was staring pointedly at her. Lifting his hand, he gave her a knowing wave. She looked down at her hands, but didn't mistake the lowed rumble of the male laughter.

That man is going to stop laughing at me.

~YH~

"This is amazing. Everything looks like so much fun. It's like a county fair." Rena walked beside Greta to the festival ground area. It was a large clearing with a playground and park at one end, the other was set up with tents, booths, field games and so much more: food, crafts and a small stage where there was a kids' talent show happening. After stopping by Gobi's Diner, where she started off eating a large garden salad, Rena ended with three homemade rolls dripping with honey and most of Greta's creamy smoked salmon pasta in her stomach. She was stuffed.

Still shocked that she could have honey, Rena waited for some kind of reaction, but none came—just a craving for more. That same hunger had led her to try a taste of Greta's fish. When nothing happened but a warm glow in a belly and a sense of euphoria, Rena had taken another forkful, then another. She would have been embarrassed by her poor manners if Greta hadn't laughed and ordered them another plate and a bowl of Gobi's hearty salmon and vegetable chowder. Which Rena recognized as tasting a lot like her grandmother's soup without the chunks of fish floating in it.

It didn't take much effort for her to deduce that if her grandmother was feeding her honey on the sly that more than likely Genma had been doing the same with the seafood. *But why?* That simple question was plaguing Rena.

"Well, this is Den County." Greta teased as she weaved them through all the activity to a booth with SHARDIK FARMS HONEYCOMBS painted across the top.

"Hi, Lola." Greta greeted the older woman inside the booth.

"Greta, are those Genma's muffins?" Lola's face was lit with a smile as she rubbed her hands together.

Rena couldn't believe that this woman sold so many honeycomb treats, but was still excited to get her grandmother's muffins.

"They sure are." Greta passed the container to Lola over the side of the stand.

"Perfect, I have a nice dish and place for them." Lola carried the muffins to the large table where a man was working and set it down.

"Have you had a chance to meet, Rena, Genma's granddaughter?"

"Oh, my goodness. You don't say." Lola turned her million-watt grin on Rena. "I haven't seen you since you were a baby. How's your mother?"

At the mention of her mother, Rena forced a smile on her mouth and hoped Lola and Greta didn't pick up on it and think it reflected on her meeting the woman. "She's fine. Living in Massachusetts."

Lola stared off in the distance for a second as she said, "Gracious, your mother and I went to school together. We used to run around this town trying to get all the handsome males to sniff after us." She laughed.

The thought of sitting down with Lola and tapping her brain about her mother's childhood was tempting to Rena. Her mother was never forthcoming about anything to do with growing up in Den County. It was as if Lillian wanted to pretend that her hometown didn't exist in her mind. Rena thought it was a shame. Evidently her mother had friends and people in the area who thought fondly of her, even if Lillian didn't feel the same about them.

"You caught me that way." A burly man in the back cutting large blocks of honeycomb into smaller pieces called out.

"Yes I did." Lola looked back over her shoulder and gave the man a wink. "Don't mind him. That big, bear of a male is my Ben."

Rena waved at the man.

"You all headed over to Fur Field to the softball game?" Lola leaned out of her booth window. "That's where Gordon and Shayna are."

"I heard about that. I'm planning to head over and see if they have any spots left," Greta replied. "You okay with that, Rena?"

"Sure. I haven't seen a good game in a while." Not to mention if she said no, Greta may take her back home and that would set Rena the one place she was trying to avoid, around Cord.

"Let's go then. Okay, Lola, Ben, we will see you two later." Greta began to move away.

"Nice meeting you, Lola...again." Rena said as she followed Greta toward the far end of the park area.

"Don't be a stranger!" Lola called out to her.

Smiling back at the former friend of her mother's, Rena didn't respond. She didn't want to make any promises to the woman.

As she and Greta headed to the field, her grandmother's neighbor pointed out different people and families they passed. Explaining to Rena what business they ran or how many offspring they had. Kids were running everywhere through the fairgrounds. No one appeared concerned and it seemed to her that they all pitched in to keep an eye on the children and elderly. Rena liked this county, with its friendliness and fairs. There seemed to be more camaraderie and support in this town then she'd seen in any city she'd ever lived in.

"There's the field." Greta pointed to the large field coming into view with groups of people gathered around.

"Is it over?" Rena lifted her hand over her eyes, shielding them as she started off in the distance about a hundred yards away.

"I hope not." Greta picked up her pace.

"Greta, perfect. We need another player." A tall man with dark brown hair waved them over.

Greta turned her fast walk into a jog.

Rena followed suit. She'd never considered how much energy she would expend when she decided to come out to the festival. This was the most exercise she had gotten in a very long time. She was happy that she didn't feel weak or exhausted yet.

"Great, Tim. I was hoping to join in." Greta explained to the brown haired man.

One of the things Rena had come to realize was that every man in Den County over the age of twenty was both extremely tall and just as bulky as Cord. She wondered what was in the water of the town to grow their men so big. She would like to bottle it and take it back to North Carolina with her.

Rena didn't miss all the men checking her out and the women eyeing her, not negatively but more out of curiosity.

"We need someone else because Shayna is breeding again so she can't play." A man standing beside the one Greta had called Tim nodded his head toward a set of bleachers where people sat watching the picking of teams happen.

"Congrats, Gordon." Greta told him then yelled a greeting in the direction of the stands.

Rena spotted a pretty dark-skinned black woman in the stands appearing to be in the middle stages of pregnancy holding her hand up and giving a finger wave.

"You all have room for one more?" Greta asked. "This is Rena, Genma's granddaughter. She's staying there for a little while. Rena this is Kaley, Natasha, Blake, Gordon, Stephen, Lacey, Marcella, John, Chris, Rand and Tim Bjorn, Cord's cousin." Greta ticked off each person in the large group.

Rena could see the family resemblance in Tim's features even though his hair was dark and Cord's was wheat blonde. The women gave her a friendly nod, but each of the men came to her and took her hand, she thought they would shake it, but instead they all seemed to bow their heads slightly and *sniff* it. She wasn't even going to attempt to decipher the odd custom.

"I don't mind at all if she joins in," Rand, a café au lait complexioned black man, announced still holding her hand.

With a tug, Rena pulled it away and took a small step back. Realizing that Greta was referring to her as the extra, Rena chimed in, "Uh, that's not necessary. Seems like you all already have an equal number with Greta, I can sit on the bench."

"Come on, Rena, you will have fun."

Shaking her head, Rena began, "I'll be fin—"

"If you don't play, Rena, then I'll have to sit out."

Cold chills of shock ran up her spine that turned into hot sparks as the sensation spread into the rest of her body. Rena didn't have to turn around to see that the deep, husky voice belonged to Cord. The man she thought she'd escaped hours ago.

"Cord!" The petite Asian woman named Marcella's eyes became extremely bright and the smile on her face almost made it from one ear to the other as she turned and saw him.

Rena almost expected the woman to start clapping and jumping up and down in a cheer of Cord's unexpected presence. The heat that previously was radiating through Rena's body settled in her stomach and seemed to cause her blood to boil at the woman's response. Disregarding both the girl and her own odd emotions, Rena slowly turned and faced Cord.

The man looked amazing in a navy blue shirt and light colored denim jeans, different from what he'd been wearing earlier when she'd left him leaning against his hoe—another white shirt and dark gray jeans.

"I thought you were working?" Rena tried to keep her tone matter of fact, neutral as if she didn't care where Cord was or what he was doing with his time.

His dark gaze was fixed on her, the look he gave her was so direct and intense she would have sworn everyone else around them had disappeared.

She had to swallow and inhale several times to keep her heart in check as it started to speed up. However, she wished she hadn't because she picked up the woodsy combination of White Fir and nutmeg—nature's erotic bouquet. It amazed her how Cord's distinct earthy spice scent could be detected by her among all the other people.

"Then it's all settled. Cord you can be on Gordon's team and I will take Rena on mine." Tim spoke up before Rena could voice further objections.

Not wanting to appear like a killjoy, Rena said, "Okay." And hoped her strength held. Passing out before everyone would be an embarrassment she could do without.

Everyone began to disperse, filing out to either one of the two benches behind home plate or to the field to take positions. However, Cord didn't go either way, instead he took a few steps toward her making the gap between them smaller. His scent enveloped her, making her mind hazy and her body tighten.

Studying her for a moment, he asked, "Are you sure you're okay...with playing?"

The assessing look he gave her was making her uncomfortable, he could possibly see too much. Personal things about herself she didn't want to reveal. Her illness had already caused one man to walk out of her life and Cord wasn't even hers. *Nor do I want him to be*. She told herself.

"Of course, why wouldn't I be?" Lifting an eyebrow she dared him to question her decision. This man didn't know her. No matter how strong her body seemed to respond to him. "It's just a simple community game of softball."

With a short shake of his head, he said, "Yes, but it can be intense to say the least. Not to mention Den residents are extremely competitive."

Never really into sports before, she considered changing her mind at his words. Last thing she wanted to do was to cost her team the game and have to worry about disappointing the new associates she had made. Proof she was the *weakest* link. Nervous, she licked her lips.

Cord must have picked up on her reaction to his

words, because he placed a wide, strong hand on her shoulder. "Don't worry about it. You'll do fine."

"Hey, Cord, you going to let her play ball or mark her?" Gordon called out from first base.

Mark me?

With a lopsided smile he winked at her then started walking away, but not before she heard him say, "Maybe both."

With a puckered brow, Rena walked to the bench where most of her teammates were waiting to bat. Marcella was in position at home plate waiting for the slow-pitch from Kaley, who occupied the mound. As soon as Cord took up the outfield position, the game was underway with a round of clapping from the people in the stands.

CHAPTER SEVEN

Almost two hours later, Cord received slaps on his back from his teammates for the grand slam he hit that took his ball well beyond the boundaries of Fur Field's fencing, lost in the Redwood forest behind it. It had brought in three other players giving his team the lead and the win. His run in was just gravy on top giving them a two point lead at the end. As the two teams filed into separate lines and shook hands as they walked past each other with the 'good game' dictum, he was glad to see that Rena, even with her earlier reluctance, had gotten into the spirit of the game.

Before the game got started, he'd sensed something with her. The concern she was feeling for whatever reason had almost been palpable. He doubted that anyone else picked up on it, she had been doing a damn good job of covering it up. However, he was too attuned to her to be fooled.

Soon, she had shaken off whatever it had been and he'd watched as she laughed and chatted with her team, making friends with everyone, excepted one person. Marcella.

Before he could make his way along the people of his cousin's team to Rena, Marcella grabbed his arm and pulled him to the side. "So, Genma's relative is staying at her house?"

Cord looked down at the white chalk line in the dirt then up at the sky and to the trees, any place but at Marcella. He didn't want to encourage her. "Yup."

"Aren't you doing some work out there...while Genma is away?"

Glancing toward the stands, he witnessed Gordon lifting his wife off the bench and kissing her. He envied the honey farmer having a life mate. Even though he'd heard that Gordon hadn't realized Shayna was his until he tracked down her scent during last year's Bear Run.

"Yup," he replied, almost positive where this conversation was going. Unable to stop himself, Cord's gaze was drawn to Rena where she stood talking to Greta and Natasha, Sheriff Smokey's receptionist. The three tall black women, striking in different ways, looked as if they should be modeling an African American fashion magazine.

"So, that leaves you and...*Rena*...a lot of time alone."

He didn't have to be genius or psychic to pick up on the jealous tone of Marcella's words.

Finally, pinning his ex-girlfriend with a stare. Now that his mate was here, the last thing he wanted was any confusion between him and Marcella that would cause more obstacles between him and Rena. He had tried to be as gentle with Marcella as possible, but, he could clearly see now he needed to be blunt. "Look,

Marcella, I'm not trying to—"

"So, you're decent at softball...a girl's game." Tim, his cousin's voice broke Cord off from his let down of Marcella.

Turning, Cord faced the man stalking toward him, still carrying his bat and baseball glove.

Arching a slow brow at Tim, Cord folded his arms across his chest wondering what his cousin was getting at. "But we won, beat your team and that was good enough for me, I don't care if we were playing jacks," Cord taunted the cocky Were-bear before him.

Tim clenched his jaw, evident in the flexing of muscles in his face.

Cord couldn't care less if his ribbing aggravated Tim. The other male had approached him. His cousin was an ass when he wanted to be and too arrogant for any one Were.

"That's no proof that you can run this town. Guide and control the people."

Cord shook his head and rolled his eyes. He should have figured everything with his cousin had to do with the mayoral seat. *When would Tim learn to let it go?* Cord had no plans to release his position to the man, no matter what anyone thought. His taking over after his father departed the office was a matter of pride and honor and Cord wouldn't see that mantle passed to anyone. Especially the supercilious ass bear shifter before him.

They were starting to draw a crowd, Cord noticed. Weres could smell two males in a pissing contest from five counties over.

"Watch me," Cord bit out.

With squinted eyes, Tim stared at him.

Cord locked gazes with him. He wasn't intimidated

by his cousin. No fucking way. It was best that Time recognized that fact now.

The first to break the eye contact, Tim glanced around him, seeing the faces of males and females gathered waiting to discover where all of this exchange was leading to. A sly smile appeared on Tim's face seconds before he said, "How about we put your Alpha-claims to the test. In a more masculine way?"

Tilting his head, he stared at Tim. "Such as?"

Holding out his hand with his baseball glove in it, Tim let the leather mitt drop.

Cord looked down at the item that had created a small dust cloud around his feet when it hit the dirt. Glancing back up to his cousin, he asked, "What the fuck is the purpose of such damn dramatics?"

Shit. No one had to tell Cord what was coming. Den County had few customs that took place in such a manner, but one.

"I challenge you to a grappling match," Tim declared loudly ensuring that anyone at Fur Field heard him issue the challenge clearly. "If you're man enough."

Cord knew that his cousin was betting on the fact that having his life mate and children would provide Tim with the strength to get the best of Cord, show him up before a captivated audience, witnesses. Cord was sure that if Tim won he'd immediately demand Cord relinquish the official seat. Cord would be damned if he let that happen.

"Cord?"

It was Rena's voice that broke into his thoughts. He wasn't sure when she'd come up on the opposite side of him than Marcella was still standing. However, he could not spare Rena the time to answer any questions she may have about the proceedings.

Instead, Cord grabbed a fistful of his shirt and yanked it over his head. Staring boldly at his cousin, he tossed the shirt to his left, where Rena stood and said, "Draw the fucking circle, Tim. Let's get to it."

His bear roared and scratched inside of him. Cord knew that his animal side wanted the opportunity to go for his cousin. But, if he allowed his bear out, Cord could guess it would shock the hell out of Rena. Not to mention he'd have to keep his bear from going for Tim's throat. This wasn't a challenge to the death, just one of dominance.

Tim gave him a sharp nod then lifted his hand high and waved his wife, who was sitting with their children in the stands, over to him. When Nita, a short, pregnant, Hispanic female got to Tim's side, his cousin handed her his bat and then removed his shirt and handed that to his life mate as well.

Collecting the bat from her, Tim ushered all the bystanders back then used the top of the bat to drag a wide circle around him and Cord. After chucking the bat toward Stephen, his cousin's good friend, Tim stepped before Cord.

With arms wide, and one foot before the other, Cord assumed the stance and demanded, "Call it, Gordon."

~YH~

Rena could not believe her eyes. Two larger than life, handsome, bare-chested men were before her in a makeshift circle locked together. She wasn't sure whether Cord had Tim, or Tim had Cord.

Their feet were planted wide in the dirt, they leaned forward toward each other. Both men's heads were buried against each other's shoulder with a thick arm secured around each neck as their other hands were gripping a wrist.

Tim squatted low then sprung upward using his knees and flipped Cord over his head bringing both men to the dirt on their backs. Rena swore the ground shook beneath the feet of all the observers by the force.

The crowd gathered around them became bigger as word of the wrestling men must have spread through the fairgrounds. She would have anticipated that someone would step in and stop them. Especially when Sheriff Smokey showed up. However, the bystanders just cheered them on.

Cord and Tim became a tangle of fast-moving arms and legs. Rena wasn't sure how she followed the blurred movement and fierce actions. When Tim attempted to swing his body over Cord and pin him to the ground, Cord must have anticipated the position because he snapped his legs up and hooked his ankles around Tim's neck. With a grunt, Cord forced him off him, slamming Tim back to the dirt.

She wasn't sure how Tim found the strength to bring his feet up to Cord's chest and kick him off. Both men scrambled to their feet back to the starting stance. The men were oblivious to anything else around them as their heels skirted the perimeter as they circled each other.

Like Titans, the brawny men clashed again. Amidst growls and roars, they tussled and wrestled with each other, Cord and Tim attempting to show their dominance.

Tense moments passed for Rena as she watched, feeling helpless to do anything. She couldn't help but concentrate all of her energy, all her inner strength to Cord. Even though she knew there was little possibility of her compelling her life force into Cord and making him stronger. However, it didn't stop her from allowing the voice that had once been small inside of her to roar Cord's name, a devout chant.

Cord. Cord. Cord.

At one with the voice within, Rena whispered, "You can do this."

"Come on, Tim. This is your time. The position is yours to take." Nita shrieked, rubbing her small protruding belly as if it was a talisman of strength for Tim.

Never one to shy away from competition, the more Nita shouted the harder Rena concentrated. Focusing in on the one man that had somehow come to mean more to her than a simple unwanted flirtation, her desire—Cord.

When Tim had Cord's shoulders pinned, bearing down on him with all of his weight, looking as if he'd bested Cord, things shifted, changed. With a sound coming from the pile of torsos and limbs that sounded practically inhuman, a roar boomed around them.

Rena realized it was Cord who had released the sound as he gripped Tim around the waist in some sort of bear hug. As if discovering a hidden well of strength, Cord began fighting with more vigor. Cord arched his back from the dirt, lifting Tim up with him.

Tim, struggling to retain his purchase on Cord, found himself rapidly rolled right and buried shoulders-deep in the dusty ground. Cord had a firm grasp around Tim's throat, Cord broad arm and full weight was pressing Tim down.

Rena had never been one to enjoy a wrestling match or boxing in the past, but as she watched these two burly men tussle around in the dirt, she found that her body was vibrating with excitement at the male display. She wanted to fan herself.

Unable to look away, she continued to watch.

No matter how Tim grunted, bucked, or twisted left to right, he could not break Cord's hold.

"Submit Tim, Cord is the victor." Sheriff Smokey pronounced in a deep, rumbling voice.

Reluctantly, Tim dropped his arms to the ground showing his submission.

Finally, having his cousin recognize his dominance, Cord released the other man. Taking a moment to consume a few deep breaths, he steadied himself. Soon he shoved up from the ground, rising to his feet, his stance wide, steady as he stared down at the beaten man.

"This is done. Over," Cord declared to Tim who was now sitting up, heaving in great gulps of air.

"Oh...Great Spirit...Cord you were...amazing." Marcella rushed to Cord's side, chest heaving as she attempted to *pant* her words out.

It wasn't the neediness in the other woman's voice or Marcella's apparent display of wantonness that made Rena feels as if she'd swallowed a cactus and its needles were digging in her stomach, but the hand. Yes, the single hand the woman lay on Cord as if she was trying to put some claim on him by her flagrant touch.

Cord glanced away from his cousin who was pushing himself up off the ground and dropped his gaze to his bicep where Marcella's hand was. Rena wasn't sure what the past or present relationship between Cord and the petite, brown-haired, Asian woman might be, nor did she wait to see how Cord responded. In an instant, before she knew what was happening Rena reacted.

Taking one, maybe two big steps forward, brought her close to Marcella. A sound started in her core, quaked up through her body and came out sounding like what Rena's ears could only describe as a growl. A low roar of warning to the other woman.

Rena couldn't figure out where or how the sound had come out of her, but it did. Her focus had tunneled and narrowed in on the other woman in a red haze. In seconds, if Marcella wasn't smart enough to heed her blatant threat, Rena was confident she'd rip the woman apart, starting with tearing the arm off that clasped Cord. A part of her wanted the Asian beauty to try her, challenge her.

Still holding Cord, Marcella's head snapped to the side and pinned Rena with a stare, and her lips curled up in a snarl.

Is she baring teeth at me?

Rena wondered, not an ounce of fear had travelled through her hot veins. She growled again and advanced closer.

"Marcella, take your hand off me." Cord didn't ask, he demanded. His voice was graveled and full of tension, and something else. This man had just proven to all who watched that he was leader of this town. He was the strongest person and ready to take on whoever was foolish enough to challenge him or stand in the way of what he wanted.

She had been impressed, turned on and proud as she'd watched his show of force over Tim. When Rena dragged her stare away from Marcella, drawn to Cord and she saw that he wasn't looking at the other woman, but at her. His gaze was intense, direct and bold. The heated look in his onyx gaze with large specks of golden flash revealed his lust and need for her.

The air between her and Cord crackled with kinetic energy.

The red haze that she'd been feeling trapped in just moments before had vanished as if blown away by a gust of wind, only to be replaced with a soft golden haze. She couldn't explain it, but it was aimed at Cord. She wanted this man. Desired him with such a fierce need and hunger, she felt consumed, blind with longing. She craved this man. More than honey or salmon.

Not waiting for Marcella to remove her hand, Cord swept the woman away like a bothersome fly as he stepped to Rena. Seizing her arm in an unbreakable grip, he led them in a brisk strut off the field.

Not caring what the scene looked like to the others left standing behind them, Rena followed. Rather she was matching Cord step for step, as if they were in a race toward pleasure. In her fist, she clutched his shirt high against her chest, taking in his heady scent as they strutted out a side gate of the field then down past the back of a few tents on the outskirts of the fairgrounds. She didn't know where Cord was taking her, but he was a man on a mission. And she was too ecstatic to be a part of whatever was coming.

Soon they reached Paw Tracks Street, the main road that ran through town where Cord made a sharp left away from the festival crowds. A few people were milling around businesses and storefronts, but a lot less compared to the crowds surrounding the park.

People stared, watched them but didn't bother to call out greetings, as Cord stormed through the street hell bent on his goal. He cut along the side of Bear & Cub Hardware store and continued until he brought them to a parking lot empty of people but full of vehicles. Like most of the town, people were parked everywhere as they drove in for the day's festival activities.

Rena spotted Cord's black extended cab pick-up at the far end. Once they got to it, he released her, allowing her to climb into the front passenger side. Making haste around the hood, he snatched his door open. She was impressed by the durability of the truck that the door didn't come flying off in his hand.

In and behind the wheel, Cord turned to face her. The flecks of gold in his eyes earlier had fully taken over his dark irises now. She wasn't sure why the anomaly happened or what it meant, but somehow she understood it had something to do with her. A reaction. And it thrilled her to see it.

She felt itchy and agitated. Her body was so turned on she thought she would lose her mind.

"I'm going to kiss you, Rena." He stared across the front bench arresting her with his gaze.

Recognizing the warning, in his words, she felt her heart rate do the impossible, start beating faster. "Do it, Cord." She wanted to be ravished by this bear of a man.

Reaching out, he pulled his shirt from her hands and tossed it to the floor of his truck. She didn't even realize she was still holding it.

Anticipating he would lean over and set his lips against hers, she was caught off guard when he took hold of her arms and hauled her onto his lap as if she weighed nothing.

Gasping, she straddled his lap. With the steering wheel behind her, there was little room, leaving her no option but to press herself close him. Something she didn't mind at all. She wanted to be up close and personal with this bear of a man. She'd never known another man *so* big, imposing and sexy as hell, that was Cord. Even seeing the other men in Den County today didn't have the same effect on her that being around Cord did.

Perched on his lap, she would have thought he would begin to kiss and maul her. Instead he just held her against him, staring into her face.

"You are so beautiful." His thumb stroked her chin causing the tip of it to graze the underside of her bottom lip. "I can't get enough of your eyes, your skin...your scent."

Oh, hell, this man could have her coming from just mere words.

"Look who's talking." She ran her hands over his hair. "I thought you were in the mood for kissing not quoting poetry," she taunted, breathless.

"Let me give the lady what she wants." Cupping the back of her head, he angled her mouth just as he wanted it. Slanting his lips on hers, he showed her the magnitude of his desire.

She felt flushed, feverish as Cord took command of her mouth. The kiss blew her mind. It was skilled, passionate and forceful. She'd never had a man demand so much from her in a simple kiss.

However, she wasn't going to play the mild submissive. Palming the back of his head, she pressed her knees out as far as she could in the confines of the truck. She ground her sex against the hard, bulge she felt beneath her.

When his tongue dipped in, she sucked it, holding it...him in her mouth.

He moved away, licking a path along the side of her

neck. In the curve of her shoulder he drew a mouthful of her skin in his mouth. And grazed her flesh with his teeth.

Something about feeling the scratch of his teeth across her flesh caused shivers to race down her spine and heat bloomed a blazing inferno in her stomach. *Bite me.*

Rena wasn't sure where that thought came from, but even as she attempted to push it away, it brought with it a vision of Cord fucking her hard and burying his teeth deep into her. She wanted to believe that she thought the image was wicked, depraved...too paranormal for it to ever happen in reality, but she didn't.

A whimpered moan came out of her mouth. Grabbing his head, she lifted it and kissed him hard until they were both panting and heaving in small gulps of air in between more kisses.

With her palms flat on his bare chest, she dug her nails into his toned muscles, loving the brush of hair that tickled her skin. She wanted to touch him in many more places.

His hands were all over her, rubbing her thighs, squeezing her ass and pinching her nipples.

"More..." Gracious she needed more of Cord in any and every way.

He tugged at her blouse, yanking it from the waistband of her jeans. When his fingers brushed her sides beneath, she whispered, "I love your big, strong hands."

"Now, who's the poet?"

She laughed and kissed his perfect mouth again.

Strange and wonderful sensations were whirling inside of her, outside of the inner voice. That was a part of her, but separate in some manner, there were other things. The golden haze to her sight had taken a back seat to another wonder, her gums behind her eye teeth were tingling. Something akin to a minor toothache was happening in her mouth. However, instead of hurting, the throbbing was pleasurable in a way to her. It made her want to sink her teeth into something...someone...Cord. Unable to resist, she nipped his bottom lip.

"Sh-i-it..." the growl that came out of him vibrated in the interior of the truck, making the warm air pulsate.

Like a man possessed, he lowered his hands and worked at her fastening. Her belt was no struggle for him. Neither were the buttons and zipper of her jeans.

The thought of stopping him never entered her mind. She wanted his hands all over her.

Slipping his hand into her panties, he cupped her sex. "Fuck, you're soaked." His eyes closed for a moment and he inhaled deep, loud. "I can smell your heat."

The way he said it didn't lend itself to her feeling embarrassed over the evidence of her need, but turned her gooey inside with excitement. Wantonly, she circled her hips and pushed against his palm, desperate for more. "It's you," she confessed. "I feel like I've been in this state all day."

"Then let *us* do something about that."

"Us?" she looked down at him, but before she could question him further about the emphasis, Cord spoke.

"Give me your hand, Rena," he demanded, his voice rough, barely audible.

Staring into those intense, hot golden eyes, she held her hand out.

Removing his hand from her pants, he linked his fingers with hers and returned their joined hands back to her pants. He guided them, used laced fingers to stroke her sex in the snug space.

~YH~

The heady scent of her mating lust was driving Cord out of his mind. His mouth was salivating and his throat was so fucking tight with need he could barely breathe. Feeling the wet, warm supple skin of Rena's pussy surrounding their combined fingers had him agitated and dancing on the edge of a cliff. One he could go over at any moment.

Not here in his fucking truck. Cord was thoroughly pissed with himself for even starting such an encounter in a confined place that he wouldn't be able to love Rena right. Fuck her properly.

Her clit was hard as a diamond and extremely sensitive. Caressing the stiff little peak he enjoyed her bucking against his engorged cock.

Claim her. Mark her.

His bear was tearing him apart inside. It wasn't one for the seduction of the act of sex, but the taking, dominating part of it.

However, Cord knew he had to do this right. Rena was fragile. Not physically, but emotionally. Even as today he'd seen her bear begin to surface, reveal itself, he wasn't sure if she was aware of the changes.

Just yesterday, she'd been so reserved and skittish to the evidence of his Were traits. But on the field he'd seen the fierce territorial anger she'd exhibited toward Marcella. Before everyone on that field, she'd practically marked him as hers.

He knew that if he didn't get Rena away from his ex, there would be bloodshed. Most likely Marcella's as loud as Rena's growl had been. When her gaze had connected with his, he'd spotted the golden threads of lust in her eyes. Something that hadn't been evident yesterday when he'd kissed her in Genma's kitchen.

No, yesterday and this morning she'd been ignorantly fighting their attraction. She'd have fared better climbing an iceberg barefoot and nude, than reigning in the mating lust of her Were.

Great Spirit, he was grateful she gave in when she did. After besting his cousin in the match, the only thing Cord wanted was to claim and mark his mate.

"I want inside you bad, Rena," he confessed.

"I want you there, too."

He shoved his finger behind hers inside the tight, opening of her pussy.

She bucked her hips and tossed her head back riding them both—milking her sex.

Increasing his tempo, finger-fucking her as deep as he could, he commanded, "Come for me, Rena. Let me feel your pussy quiver in our hands."

"Cord…" her voice was rough and low, as she slammed herself against them, taking what she needed.

Dragging her shirt up and freeing one breast from the bottom of her bra, he only allowed himself a moment to admire the sienna-brown skin with its blackberry center. Opening his mouth wide he sucked in as much of her breast as he could and caressed the erect tip with his tongue. When the peak was sufficiently raised, he scraped against it with his incisor. Not enough to break the skin, yet.

Rena exploded. Screaming, she dug her nails deep into his shoulders and climaxed.

Leaning back, he watched her, seeing the light sheen of sweat coating her skin and pleasure giving her skin a rosy tint making her brown skin even lovelier.

The after-spasms coursing through her sex happened around her hand. "I can't wait to taste your pussy, sweetheart."

Lowering her head, she opened her eyes and gazed at him. "Why wait." Pulling her hand from her pants she painted his lips with her cream.

Her bold, beguiling act was almost enough to shove him over that cliff of sexual insanity. His tongue darted out and he followed her finger, tasting the savory honey of her sex. Nothing had ever tasted as good as the flavor of Rena's pussy. The only thing that could be better was him being able to drink it from the source.

Capturing her finger, he sucked it. Swirling his tongue along the lines, curves and creases, he cleaned every drop from her skin.

Moaning, she used her free hand to drag him away from her sex and licked him from wrist to the tip of his middle finger without breaking eye contact.

Fucking hot. He groaned.

When she pressed his finger into her mouth and sucked him, giving him wild visions of her mouth wrapped around his cock, a wave of ecstasy made his blood sing.

"Shit," he growled. Not from pain, but from pleasure as Rena grazed the pad of his middle finger with the extend point of one of her teeth.

Shocked, Rena jerked back and eyed the small drop of blood.

His heart was racing, while in human form the only two manifestation of their Were gene rose to the surface and both of those things were for one single purpose — mating. The first was the golden reflection of their eyes when their mating lust was incited, the other was their incisors dropped. The latter was to mark one's mate. As they matured, a Were-bear learned how to control the extension of his teeth, only releasing them when they were going to bite.

"It seems I've cut you somehow." Her brows were puckered in confusion.

Arching an eyebrow at her, he glimpsed the sharp points of her teeth. Evidently, she was oblivious to them being out. If the moment hadn't been so serious, he would have laughed. Instead, he remained still and silent, wanting to see what she would do. He would heal fast, if she did nothing, but there was a way to speed that healing process up. But he wouldn't tell her. If she didn't react in the traditional way of mates, he would be fine.

She studied it for a second. He could almost see the thoughts playing across her features as she tried to figure out what she should do.

Bringing it slowly to her mouth, she kissed it.

He held his breath, hearing the pounding of his own heart like a ceremonial drum beat in his ears.

When her pink tongue slipped from her lips and swirled around the injury, licking the cut before she drew it back into her mouth, a firecracker inside his brain exploded.

"Re-naaaa…" he growled low, whispering her name on a sigh of pleasure.

It was like no lust he'd ever experienced before. The world around him spun and drowned him into a vortex of colors and sensations to the point he found it hard to breath or think and every fiber of his being was centered at one point — Rena.

Pulling his finger out, she looked at it and smiled.

"All better now."

The cut on his finger had closed, but there was a small scar that he knew would never go away. Even healed it throbbed, pulsed. Rena had marked him. Whether she was aware of what she had done or not she'd just started their life mate bond — two more bites remained.

Fisting her hair, he pressed her body to his and kissed her, deep and unrestrained. Everything that had transpired between them until this point was a prequel to the raw passion that awaited them.

When he broke the kiss, they were both panting. If he could have, he would have driven them away with her still riding his lap, but a glimmer of reason flashed in his mind. "We're getting out of here, now." He wasn't sure if his words had even come out as a language or a series of grunts as he lifted her away from him.

Thankfully, Rena seemed to comprehend what he was attempting to communicate, because she scrambled to her seat.

Barely seeing her safely in the passenger seat, he pulled his keys out of his pocket and gunned the engine of his truck. He had to flip on the defrost to clear the front window, which had fogged over completely from the heat of their foreplay. Before his next breath he had the truck backed up then shifted to drive and tore out the parking lot behind the hardware store.

With the main road into town blocked off, he had to take the back roads to his house, extending their drive by twelve minutes, but he would do his damnedest to reduce it to five. He wanted his mate and time was not his friend at the moment.

He drove like a madman. His vision was so golden, if Sheriff Smokey knew he'd probably pull Cord over and give him a ticket for driving while lustfully intoxicated. But the law man would have a chase on his hands, because Cord didn't plan to stop his truck until he'd reached his house and he could have Rena on whatever place they got to first. Nothing but death would keep him from fucking her, now.

CHAPTER EIGHT

Rena's heart was beating so hard she felt dizzy and lightheaded. However, she didn't feel like she was going to pass out, but full of energy...and lust. That was the only word she could use to describe the kaleidoscope of desire inside of her. It wasn't pretty, or sweet or kind. It was base and crude, giving her a tunneled vision with Cord at the end of her sights. It was taking every ounce of her strength not to crawl back across the seat and straddle him again. This time she'd pull his cock from his pants and ride it hard.

Unable to stop herself, she stared at the deliciously handsome man sitting beside her. His face was tight and his hands were fisting the steering wheel so tight, she was surprised it didn't bend. She didn't have to be told that his need for her was just as strong, she could feel it inside her. She wasn't sure how, but it was as if there was a part of him in her, connecting them. She knew it didn't make sense, but the impression was there still the same.

She allowed her gaze to travel along those well-defined muscles of his arms until she was eyeing the thick bulge beneath the fly of his jeans.

"Rena, if you don't stop staring at my dick, I'm going to pull this truck over and fuck you on the hood."

"You don't hear me arguing against that idea do you?"

Cord slammed on the brake and the bed of the truck fishtailed once before he brought it under control. She wasn't sure what had possessed her to bait a beast, but she couldn't help it, she was feeling so alive.

He pinned her with a hard gaze, a warning. His eyes were liquid gold. She could barely see his pupils.

His nostrils flared as he took a deep breath before refocusing on the path before them. He grunted, or growled or roared indecipherable words as he pressed on the gas pedal again and shot them down the road.

She smiled as she rolled her window down and enjoyed the crisp fall breeze coming into the window. Catching the blurred view of the tall, thick redwoods as their branches reached high in the sky she wanted to get out of the truck and run through them. In forty-eight hours something had changed in her.

Honey, fish and Cord, three things she believed she shouldn't have. Three things that weren't good for her. However, they were the three things that had awakened a hibernating animal inside her core. It was as if she'd never truly lived until she'd arrived back in Den County.

Where has your life been headed all this time, Rena.

Right here.

Just yesterday she'd been thinking that since she was feeling better, she would be able to go home and get her old job back. She peeped at Cord and knew that she'd need to do some serious re-evaluating of her life.

Slowing the truck, barely, Cord turned onto a dirt path. The driveway led to a cabin that was very different from her grandmother's. It was spread wider, taking up a larger area of the forest with a second floor. The lawn around it was so well manicured and trimmed she would have sworn someone cut it by hand with a pair of shears. Instead of a wraparound porch like her grandmother's, it was complimented by flagstone walkways and patio. It was definitely all male. There wasn't a single flower around the home to make it 'pretty.' This was a breathtaking, but masculine domain.

Screeching to a halt, Cord shut off the truck then jumped out. At her door, he yanked it open. She thought he would take her hand and help her out the vehicle but he stood back as if he were afraid to touch her.

Sliding out of the big truck, she stood before him.

"My house is unlocked. My bedroom is upstairs. Wait for me there. I suggest if there is any piece of clothing you're wearing that you don't want ripped to shreds you remove it before I get there."

The tension in his body was almost palpable. She couldn't help but notice the death grip he had on the passenger side door.

Figuring he needed a little space, and time, she gave him a sharp nod then stepped around him, ensuring she didn't brush against him. Walking up the stone path, she didn't allow herself to look back at him.

She didn't want him to see the pleading look in her eyes. Now that she was more than an arm's reach away from Cord she could feel the nervousness in her core.

She wondered if he was second guessing being with her. Things had gone so fast since the softball game. Maybe they were rushing things.

The thought that she should go back to the truck and ask him to take her back to her grandmother's house, rose in her mind. However, it was quickly overtaken by the need still bubbling in her core.

Not to mention the voice inside of her yelling 'no'.

At the front door of the cabin, she turned the handle and entered the dwelling. In his living room there was a long couch that sat before a state-of-the-art flat screen SMART television including surround sound equipment. Similar to her grandmother's cabin, there were shelves filled with more movies than a video store. Shutting the door behind her, she moved deeper into the room and saw the two high back chairs that sat before his fireplace and a chess set on a small table between them.

Not interested at the moment in touring the rest of the house, she followed Cord's directions and took the stairs to the second level — a loft with a smaller couch and television was there with a second, smaller fireplace. It overlooked the living room downstairs.

At the far end of the area was an archway. Beyond it she could see a large bed, bigger than any king-size bed she'd ever seen. Four adults could probably sleep comfortably in it without touching the person beside them. Once she was in the room, she took in the cinnamon and emerald decorations. There was a dresser with a mirror, plus a nightstand, but not many other things to clutter the space. The only other door besides the bathroom was the one that led to a patio with a breathtaking view of the woods.

Turning back to the bed, she found herself

transfixed by the painting on the wall above his bed. It was of a river that appeared to be the one that ran through Den. However, the section of it that was captured in the frame was a dock similar the one at the end of her grandmother's property.

From the view of the artist, the dock seemed both within reach yet too far away to truly touch. There was something about the scene that tugged at her heart and made it ache. Then she noticed the signature in the corner, Genma B. Her grandmother was the artist. Taking a deep breath, she released the emotion and refocused on her task at hand. Even with the momentary separation from Cord, she still wanted him.

Not really caring about her clothing, she removed them mainly to prove to him how much she desired him. Tomorrow may bring a about a conversation they needed to have about what all this meant, but tonight she just wanted to feel.

~YH~

Cord felt like he was about to come out of his skin — literally and figuratively. He didn't want to send Rena away, but his bear was too close to the surface. Cord feared that if he didn't let him out it would cause him to tear down his own house fucking Rena. Not that the human male part of him saw that as an issue, he wanted her just as bad as his bear wanted to mark her.

But, Cord needed to quell the madness just a little. Moving to the back of his cabin, he shed his remaining clothes quickly and shifted with a simple thought letting his bear free. For a moment his bear paused and glanced at the door that led into his kitchen, but Cord nudged him and sent him on his way.

No more than ten minutes later, he was back at his

home. Reclaiming his human form, he gathered his clothing and shoes and entered the kitchen. Dropping the stuff in the laundry room, he moved through his kitchen to get to the steps that would lead him to his room. To Rena.

Even though she'd only been in his house a short while, her scent was already woven into the fabric of his home. The run had calmed him some, but it had not removed the desire he had for her. Nothing could do that.

At the archway of his bedroom, he considered heading to his shower first, removing some of the sweat covering his body and possibly helping to balance him a little more.

"Every time I smell the woodsy scent of white fir and nutmeg it brings the image of you to my mind...erotic, hot images of you that will incite my blood and warm me from the core out."

Her gaze had been fixed on something beyond the window and he'd believed her unaware of his presence. However, it was a foolish thought with her Were senses kicking into full gear. A bear shifter could locate their mate anywhere. Rena had tagged him and that knowledge almost brought him to his knees.

Inhaling deeply then exhaling, he observed her. His mate. She was a beguiling beauty lounging nude in the center of his big bed. Her thick, ebony curls were spread across his pillows. Passing the arch, he allowed his gaze to travel lower on her body. Taking in the sight of places he had touched in his truck but not seen.

Her high full breasts were drawn tight at the tips. "Are you cold?"

Bringing her gaze around to him, she smiled, her eyes still golden. "No." The heat in her stare let him know that it was desire that caused her nipples to tighten.

Continuing his perusal, he took in her narrow waist and flared hips. Ready to take in the bare seat of her womanhood, something caught his eye. Glancing to the right of her sex and resting above her hipbone he saw a mark.

Catching his stare, she looked down. "My birthmark. It's a little odd shaped but it's where I get my nickname, Red."

Gazing at the mark that was as red as a ripe strawberry, he didn't find it weird, but *remarkable*. It was a small replica of a bear paw. "Does everyone in your family have a similar marking?"

She shook her head. "Nope, just me." Wrinkling her nose, she peeped down at it again. "I knew a girl in college that had a birthmark on her knee in the shape of a heart. I always thought it was better than whatever this is supposed to be."

Cord didn't agree. Raising his gaze, he looked into her eyes and he shook his head. "Yours is perfect. In some way it's a symbol of who you really are."

Laughing, she said, "I'm not sure how something that looks like the Hawaiian Islands can mean anything, but okay."

Standing, at the foot of the bed, he beckoned her to him with a finger. "Come here, *Red*, and I'll do my best to show you before the sun rises tomorrow."

"Hmm." She rose to her knees and moved down the bed to him. "I'm more than willing to let you show me whatever you like, tonight."

"Later, I will remind you of your words." He winked at her.

Leaning down, he kissed the red mark then swirled

his tongue over the imprint, tracing it. Once he was sufficiently satisfied that he'd covered all of it, he dragged his tongue up her side, which he discovered was a tickle spot for her. Continuing on, he tasted the underside of her breast and traveled around it until he got to her nipple. Placing a kiss there, he moved upwards along her collar bone and neck until he got to her mouth.

Without touching her anywhere else, he kissed her. Reacquainting himself with her taste. It only took a moment for his lust to resurface in full force as if he hadn't just gone for a run to calm himself.

With a growl, he broke off the kiss. "I want to taste your sweet pussy, Red Rena."

He witnessed the shuttered breath she took as she kneeled before him.

"Do you want me to touch myself again?"

Hell, yes. It was his turned to shutter from the heat flaming his blood. "Not at the moment. Turn around and put your hands on the bed."

Facing the head of the bed, she placed her hands on the mattress positioning herself on all fours. Giving him a saucy smile over her shoulder, she asked, "Like this?"

Yes. His bear growled within him.

I like it a lot. Cord and his bear agreed. No matter how many sexual positions there were, this one would always be the main one all male Were-bears desired above all others.

Instead, he said, "Lower."

She dropped to her elbows, still staring at him.

"Lower."

Her look became more beguiling as she not only stretched her arms out before her, bringing her upper body down to her shoulders, but she dipped her back so that her ass was curved high.

Staring at the plump, round, brown skin of her backside displayed before him, he had the urge to bow his head and sink his teeth into it, sharing the second mark as life mates. He resisted the act, barely. Using his hands, he pressed against the inside of her knees until she was spread wide with her pussy on exhibit before him.

Cream-coated brown folds were a gateway to the pink glistening slit beckoning him. He stepped up until his thighs bumped up against the thick mattress. Kneeling so that his nose was right at the beautiful vision before him, he drew closer and inhaled. Her spicy ambrosia was a titillating treat. Closing his eyes he strictly went with his olfactory sense — marking his soul with her bouquet.

He groaned.

"Touch me, Cord...*please*." She pleaded.

Opening his eyes, he saw her arch just a little higher, wiggling her ass before him. No longer able to hold off the desire to have her, he set his tongue at the dip at the top of her clit. He licked up in a broad sweep collecting the nectar of her pussy, not stopping until he was up past the crease of her ass, then he started again.

Once, twice...he lost count after his eighth swipe. Rena's taste was perfect, he could bury his tongue in her sex all night long and begin again the next day. Taking hold of her ass, he squeezed it and held her in the angle he wanted her as he pulled her cheeks and sex wider and rejoiced as she trembled in his hands.

"Oh....Cord...Cord," she whimpered and chanted his name as she bucked backward against his face.

Swirling his tongue around her clit, he sucked the

stiff nugget between his lips and flicked it.

When her cries started to build to words and phrases that were little more than moans and grunts, he pulled away wanting her on at the door of an orgasm, but not going through it.

She slapped her hands on the bed repeatedly, in frustrated excitement.

Licking up and down her slit, he teased her, not touching her clit or entering her sex.

"Plllease…" She forced the one word out.

Yielding to her pleas, he pressed his tongue into the heart of her pussy and caressed her walls. He stroked the warm, slick skin discovering as many dips and curves as he could reach.

Pulling away, he captured her clit once more. This time he didn't let up until she was coming.

Shaking violently, a cry, loud and hoarse, broke from her and filled the room.

Even as she was still held in the throes of ecstasy, he pushed her higher up the bed until there was room for him to climb up behind her. In less time than the instant it took him to shift, Cord was pushing inside of her.

Rena's body was still quivering from her explosive orgasm, but he shoved deep into a placed that would only be his for the rest of their life.

"Yes," she canted her hips back taking him further through her tight walls.

As a bear shifter, he knew that he was bigger than all human men. Not only in height and width of his shoulders but in the thickness and length of his cock, but she was his mate and he knew she could accommodate him.

Pulling out, he entered her again. Holding her hips,

he continued to work himself into her until she'd taken all of him. The lips of her pussy pressed against his base.

Once there, he stilled his movements. As if of one accord, Rena paused as well. They both remained in the calm, the silence and enjoyed their union.

However, his bear wouldn't give him more than seconds of peace before he was clawing and demanding Cord take her hard and mark her.

His bear wouldn't settle for anything but his claim on his mate.

Neither would he.

Withdrawing briefly, he slammed back into her and began loving her—fucking her. Over and over he pounded into her as she dug her nails deep in his mattress and thrust in time with him.

"Yes-yes-yes-yes...Cord, doo-nnn't stop. Don't fucking stop."

Never. The word exploded in his mind, his throat too tight to speak any further. His upper and lower canines were out, in place and ready. The saliva was pooling in his mouth even as his need for release was boring down on his gut, both preparing for her marking.

Sliding one arm around her waist, he brought her up until her back caressed his chest. Sweeping her curly, wild, black hair to the side, he bared her shoulder to him.

"Cord?" his name was a question, a slight hesitation from her.

However, it wasn't enough to stop him, he and his bear were too far gone and there was only one goal and they would see it through.

Curling his lips back, he dropped his head and sank

his teeth into the firm trapezius muscle availed to him. Instead of pulling away, she brought her hand up to the back of his head, holding him to her. The simple gesture welled up so many emotions inside him and caused the back of his eyes to burn.

~YH~

Rena screamed. The sound was torn from her, a blend of shock, disbelief and pleasure. Somehow in the instance before Cord bit her, she'd known what was going to happen. However, too late to stop it, she received it. Going beyond her own comfort zone, she wanted and took all the he had to offer.

Her satisfaction was toppling over beyond any ecstasy she'd ever experienced before. Cord hadn't stopped thrusting his thick cock deep inside of her, throughout the entire act of biting her. Holding his head, she slid her other hand along his arm around her waist and linked her fingers with his as her third orgasm of the evening began to reach its peak.

At the peak of her pleasure, a vision unfolded before her eyes. The water in the painting before her flowed, small waves rolling along and splashing against the posts of the dock. However, unlike before, the dock wasn't empty. There were two mature bears at the end of it, brown and one slightly bigger than the other.

Behind her, Cord gasped.

Had he seen it too?

She blinked and the bears were gone and the water motionless.

Us.

This time the voice she heard was different than the one in her core. It was deep and rough, male...Cord. *Could he see he see what I saw? How can I hear him?* Too many questions to think about, now. She shoved them into the back of her mind to ponder at a less amorous time.

Needing something, something she couldn't explain to give her that final push she was working toward she received it at the feeling of Cord's agile tongue gliding over the tender flesh of her shoulder.

Her sex squeezed his hard length, full and stretched, she came.

Thrashing against him, she celebrated as she felt the warmth of Cord's seed coating her walls as he released a sound akin to a roar behind her.

Releasing her waist, he allowed her to drop to the bed. When she rolled to her back and stared up at the impressive male before her, he took her breath away. Broad shoulders, sharp cut muscles, rippling abs, narrowed hips all directed her gaze to one place, his meaty cock. Still hard and proud as if he hadn't just found his own ecstasy. However, she wasn't shocked, because her own stamina had her sex aching for him again.

"I'm not done with you, Red." His voice was husky and rough.

Sitting up, she took hold of his cock. "Good to know since I have a few plans of my own for you."

With no further warning, she took his hard length into her mouth. She sighed with her own satisfaction at the combined taste of him and her along her tongue and the feel of his hands buried in her hair, his finger pressed firmly against her scalp.

Feeling the barely harnessed passion of her man was all the encouragement she needed.

CHAPTER NINE

Awake, Rena kept her eyes closed as she took account of her body. Every muscle was achy and her sex tender, but Rena had never felt more satisfied than she did following a night with Cord. They'd made love so many times, in so many positions and places in his cabin she was amazed that it was still standing. They'd gone down for a late night snack and she'd found herself spread out on the kitchen table with Cord over her drizzling rivers of honey on her before he licked it off. She'd happily returned the favor on her knees in the center of his kitchen. When they'd followed that feeding frenzy up with a shower, he had taken her against the wall, her breasts pressed onto the cool tile with warm water running over her and a hot man thrusting into her. Finally, she'd boldly dragged him out onto the bedroom patio where she rode him under the moonlight with the crisp breeze caressing their skin. At some exhausted point, Cord had carried her into the room and tucked them both in bed where he held her until she fell asleep. Now, all those memories caused joy to flood her core and spread warmth throughout her body making her smile.

Snuggling closer to him, her mind couldn't help but consider what life would be like with Cord. As she lay there thinking about them, she couldn't get the vision of those bears on the dock out of her mind. Just wanting a few more moments of peace before she had to face the world and even her own questions, she took a deep breath and gathered her man's natural musk. She truly did love how he smelled. However, this morning his scent was the same but different. More pungent, earthy and unrefined. But it didn't deter her from snuggling closer to him and enjoying hearing the strong rhythm of his heartbeat.

Something was tickling her nose. She moved her head, but the tickling was there too. Opening her eyes to discover, what it was, she saw nothing but fur. Thick light brown fur. She blinked, trying to clear her vision, but when she looked again it was still there.

Had it been cold last night? Did Cord put a bear skin blanket on the bed?

Leaning away, she was prepared to locate him under the mound of fur and awaken him, then the fur covered body shifted and the darkest pair of coal eyes were staring at her. A bear, not a man.

Frozen, not wanting to make any sudden movements, she watched it stretch and yawn. The sight of over thirty teeth less than a foot away from her face, kept her still.

Oh, shit? She reacted instantly as fear ran through her veins, chilling her core.

Scrambling backwards off the bed, she tried to get as far away from it as possible without taking her eyes off the massive animal. When her back hit the wall, she sat there attempting to figure out her best chances of escape. There wasn't a single weapon close at hand.

Oh, my God where is Cord? Did it eat him?

On the bed still, the bear sat up on his haunches and stared at her.

She stared back.

He advanced, not coming off the bed yet but moving to the edge.

She pressed further into the wall, wishing the wall would just open up and swallow her, before she was swallowed by a ferocious beast.

The big bear titled its head and eyed her, as if she was the strange one in the room.

He's probably trying to figure out what part of me he wants to start chewing first, Rena thought. Her chest felt tight, she tried to take a steady breath to keep her mind clear to plan an escape.

When he leaned forward as if he was going to come over the side of the bed, she screamed. A sound that came out more as a broken whimper.

Stopping, his gaze met hers again and she would have sworn there was something in his eyes that almost looked like concern.

But that's impossible. Why would this bear be concerned about his prey?

Then before her eyes, something happened. There was a shimmering of his fur and the next thing she knew Cord was sitting on the bed in its place.

What in the hell was happening? Oh, God, I must still be sleeping and I'm dreaming. That was the only explanation that made sense on why a bear was Cord/Cord was a bear. Feeling lightheaded, she closed her eyes and took in several breaths.

Please let me wake up or open my eyes and see that I'm still snuggled in bed beside Cord.

"Rena, it's okay."

Hearing his voice, she sighed and lifted her lids. However, when she did nothing had changed. He was still on the edge of the bed staring at her like she was a skittish kitten. She shook her head, feeling another scream starting to well up.

"Sweetheart, it's not a dream." His voice was low, cautious. "I'm a bear...a shifter."

Her head shook hard. *No.* He was either crazy or she was having a full blown meltdown brought on by her year-long illness. Hell maybe her mother was correct, she *was* allergic to honey and seafood, but it didn't cause hives but insanity.

Please someone direct me to the nearest mental institution.

Leaning forward, he slipped his feet to the floor at the side of the bed. "I need you to listen to me. Calm down."

Oh, hell no, this was not a calm down moment, but a get the fuck out of dodge moment. Taking her own advice she started edging slowly toward the archway of his room.

"Stop, Rena!" he commanded.

Angry at his tone, she snapped her head in his direction and pinned him with a look.

"I didn't want you to find out this way..." Frustrated, he rubbed his hands back and forth over his hair. "It's not uncommon after a night like we had that our bears take over while we sleep to help restore our strength. I need you to change so we can talk." He rose, standing.

He was speaking gibberish, nonsense. *Change? Oh,*

don't worry buddy, I plan to get my clothes on and leave. She scooted closer to the exit.

"I didn't want to do it this way but I'm not the only shifter in the room. Look at your hands."

My hands? What is he trying to pull –

Her thoughts broke off as she glanced down. Before her eyes weren't her hands as she had expected, but paws. Large brown paws covered in fur. As her gaze continued to travel along the strange form she seemed to be encased in, she saw a great girth.

No, no, no, no... The sound ripped from her chest was a half cry/half whine.

This wasn't any kind of dream, this was a nightmare. She needed to get out of here. Turning, she bolted.

"Rena!"

She refused to stop. Instead of heading through the archway she raced to the patio doors still wide open from their lovemaking session there last night. Not concerned that she was on the second floor, she launched herself over the railing.

Sailing through the air, her paws hit the ground with a thud. She felt a jolt in her muscles from the impact, but uninjured she kept moving. Sprinting into the woods she ran, no thought to where she was going she just needed to get far away from this bearman...from herself.

"Reennnaa!"

There was an agony in his voice that squeezed at her hurt, but she kept up the fast pace through the woods.

~YH~

Seeing his life mate jump from his porch and run away from him, Cord vaulted into the air and shifted

138

mid-flight. He was running the instant his four large paws hit the ground.

Shit. This was not how he had seen this day going. He'd wanted to awaken Rena with slow loving then hold her and slowly explain about their kind. Yesterday, she'd started exhibiting all of her Were traits, but he never anticipated that they would shift during the night. That she would shift. He'd told her right about why they'd taken on their bear form, but now he had to get her to calm down and listen to him so that he could guide her into shifting back.

Keeping his mate in sight, he raced through the woods for miles, following her lead. She ran in an odd pattern, going first in one direction only to zigzag around and head the opposite way. He knew she was confused. She didn't know these woods and had no clue where she was going. Finally, she arrived at the river. He saw her look from left to right, then lift her snout in the air deciding on a direction.

He figured she'd picked up a familiar scent, her grandmother's cabin. He kept the distance between them wide so that she was far enough away that she wouldn't spook and end up doing something that may get her hurt, like running into the road. Even that thought caused his gut to ache. He needed to have faith in them. They'd work this all out.

They had to.

When he finally arrived at Genma's home, Rena was standing by the front door whining and pawing the handle. It broke his heart to see her struggle to get inside the only place that was a safe haven for her.

Approaching slowly, he waited until she saw him and then he shifted. Letting her see the simplicity of the action.

Her crying grew louder and her scratching at the door more urgent.

"Rena, I need you to listen to me." He moved in closer.

The door opened with Genma standing in the opening. "Rena...?"

Unsure, he saw Rena edge back from her grandmother.

Genma was joined by his grandmother. Octavia looked past the bear on the porch to him. "Cord, what's going on? What happened?"

How was he supposed to explain the last two days to his grandmother and her best friend? With all of his concentration and focus centered on Rena he had missed his grandmother's dark green SUV parked in the driveway. Exhaling he knew this was not the time to be concerned with anyone but Rena.

"Red, come inside—" Genma began.

"No!" he barked, he needed to see this through. When Genma and his grandmother eyed him, both women with their hands on their hips looking like they were ready to issue out lectures, he said, "Give me a moment."

Moving to the steps, he gazed up into the scared eyes of his life mate. He had to do this. She may not want to be anywhere around him, but if he walked away now, there may never be a chance for him to win her trust.

"Red, sweetheart, I know you're confused and afraid." He spoke low, keeping all the tension he felt coiled along his spine out of his voice.

She glanced toward the woods. He thought she would bolt again, but she slowly returned her gaze back to him.

"You can retake your human form, the first time you do it...it will feel odd, strange and your bear may try to fight the shifting, but you can do it. I know you can." It broke his heart to know that Rena had been so unprepared for this moment. Why her family hadn't told her who she was, what she was, he didn't understand.

Her multicolored eyes still locked on him, he continued. "I need you to imagine yourself. Your human form. See your long thick ebony curls and your beautiful limbs and sienna-brown skin that's smooth, supple and lovely."

He noticed the slight shimmer around her. It started and stopped, but he could tell she was trying hard to follow his words.

He was thankful the two older women stood in silence, allowing him this time to help his mate alone.

Continuing to guide her through her first shift, he went on. "See your oval face with its perfect nose and wide, full mouth. Your high breasts and the sensuous curve of your hips that flow beguilingly into the thick thighs that a man could find solace between."

One final quiver of her fur and his Rena was sitting on the porch before him. Tears were running down her face. Those eyes that had been hazel were still. Not the trademark onyx. He wanted to reach out and pull her in his arms.

Before he could, Genma squatted down beside her and helped her to her feet then wrapped her supportive arms around her. "It will be okay, Rena. Grandmother is here."

Burying her face in her grandmother's shoulder, Rena's cries became louder.

The sound racked his soul. He wished he'd been the

one she'd turned to.

When she was led into the cabin out of his sight, Cord moved his gaze to his grandmother. So many questions rolled around in his head.

Octavia moved to the top step. "Cord, you should come in. We all need to talk."

He shook his head. "Not now, Nana. I'm the last person she wants to see. You all take care of her." Turning, he headed back toward the lake path then stopped and glanced over his shoulder. "Nana, I'm not sure what the story is here. Why Rena was sequestered away from her Were identity, but she should have some answers. The truth."

With a slow nod, his grandmother held his gaze. "She'll have it."

Inhaling, he shifted and took off. He dragged his bear away from the one place he wanted to be, with his life mate. However, Cord knew this was not the right time. He just hoped that this wasn't the last time he saw Rena like when they were younger and she'd been ripped from him.

That thought shot an arrow of pain into his heart causing his paws to stumble. Even as apprehension gripped his heart, he had to believe in them.

CHAPTER TEN

Opening her eyes, the first thing Rena did was glance at her hands. Relief showered down on her mind. Still human. Unsure of how long she'd been asleep, she pushed her body into a sitting position. She was in her room at her grandmother's house. Waking up without Cord caused her heart to ache, but there were too many questions that lay between them for her to seek him out. She needed to discover who she was. Get truth were there had been an abundance of lies.

Not wanting to play the convalescent any further, she tossed the covers away and got up. In the bathroom she washed her face and paused as she saw that there was a different set of eyes that stared back at her. All her life she'd seen her own reflection and had seen hazel eyes, the same color as her father's looking back at her, but no longer. Her irises were still hazel, but there were flecks of red in them. A color that had not been there before she'd taken a bear's form. She noted it wasn't the same coal black as her mother's, her grandmother's, Cords or everyone else's in Den County. She wondered if they would become golden like Cord's did when he desired her. One clue, their eyes, had been staring back at her this whole time and she'd missed it. What else have I missed?

Brushing her teeth, she opened her mouth wide and checked them. Everything seemed to be the same. Then she recalled the situation in the truck with Cord, the cut on his finger and how she'd had the instinct to place it in her mouth to heal it.

Just the thought of what happened made her gums tingle and a small burn started around her teeth. When she opened her mouth again she saw them, six of her teeth had extended in length.

Incisors. Canines. Confirmed the voice that had been speaking to her since she'd arrived in Den.

She knew what that voice was now, her *bear*. An animal that was a part of her, but held its own identity at the same time.

Seeing her bear's teeth and thinking of the cut on Cord's finger, her mind flashed an image of her and him making love. Recalling his strong arms around her as he thrust deep inside her sex while his teeth sank into her shoulder, her body shuddered. She'd thought he was giving her a deep hickey. Twisting to the side, she looked at her right shoulder and sure enough there was a bite mark there. Healed but very visible.

Unsure how to get her teeth to retract at first, she stood there then recalled Cord's calm voice telling her to imagine how she wanted to change. Trying it again, she pictured her human teeth and was impressed with herself when the sharp points were gone.

She needed answers. Quickly, she showered and dressed in a blouse and jeans. Leaving the room, she went in search of her grandmother. She located her and Octavia in the living room sipping tea.

"Good morning, Rena." Turning to gaze at her as she approached, her grandmother greeted her, softly.

"Hello, Rena." Octavia nodded, a kind smile on her face.

Rena didn't care for the look either woman was giving her, as if they thought she was fragile and may fall apart at any moment. It was how her mother had always treated her.

"I want to talk, and when I'm finished with my questions I need to go into town," she explained.

"Okay, please sit." Her grandmother pointed to the vacant seat on the couch that was closest to her.

Octavia had been curled up on the far end, but she rose. Walking over to Rena, she took hold of her shoulders. "You look wonderful. I'm so glad you're better. Now, I can leave."

Frowning, Rena asked, "How long have I been asleep?"

Cord's grandmother cupped her face. "Just since yesterday morning. But, I'm sure you and your bear needed that time to align."

Having to take her word for it, Rena just stared at the sympathetic woman. "You don't have to leave. I don't think any of my questions would come as a shock to you."

"Probably not. However, I have some business of my own to take care of at the moment." Kissing her on the cheek, Octavia walked over to Genma and hugged her best friend.

Genma rose and escorted Octavia to the door, her arm around her friend's waist as they walked. "I appreciate you staying until she woke."

"Of course, I promised I would help care for her. We both have some explaining to do. I'll talk to you soon." Octavia pulled the door open.

Genma waved her friend away, then closed the door.

Rena felt too agitated to sit, but she did it anyway. She needed to show her control over her emotions. Even though inside she felt like a cherry bomb had been let off inside of her and was spinning around waiting to explode.

"Seeing the color of her eyes, I think it goes without saying that Octavia is the same thing as you are."

"As *we* are." Her grandmother emphasized.

Rena understood the message loud and clear. Shaking her head she sighed. This was something she *had to* come to terms with. She was no longer the same. Hell, she had never been who she thought she was, anyway.

Tilting her head, her grandmother gazed at her, sharply assessing Rena's eye color. "Unique coloring, but fitting. I believe your birthmark, a bear paw, was a deeper marking, probably because you're a half-blood."

A bear paw. Rena had never even considered that's what the odd red shape on her hip was. Another clue on her own body she had missed. Staring into the empty fireplace, Rena asked, "Where do Weres come from? How did we start this transition?"

"We've always been a part of the world, since the Great Spirit created the Earth. Just like there are different races, size and shapes of people and species and animals in the world, there are shifters. Of all kinds."

"What?" Rena turned to face her grandmother.

"There are Weres that aren't bears?"

"Yes, lions, wolves, panthers, tigers…in India there is even a breed of Elephant shifters."

That was news to Rena. She felt as if she had been living in a sheltered vacuum. "I never knew. No one ever talks about it…on the news or magazines. Not in reality outside of movies and shows that dramatize everything." She'd been a part of making some of those local fictional shows for kids. *What a fool I had been.*

"That's how it should be. It can be unsafe for us when we remain for long periods of time away from our own communities."

"I'm sure humans would like to put us in labs to experiment on us and freak shows for entertainment." Rena mumbled, out of sorts by what she was discovering.

"Very true, unfortunately. FYI, just so you know, a lot of those television and Hollywood productions are written and created by a San Fernando Valley bobcat shifter. He does it purposely to make our species of people seem so outlandish that humans will think we are nothing but myth and fantasy."

"Good cover. Hide in plain sight."

"Yes, it is." Her grandmother eyed her, her wise gaze steady. Stepping to the coffee table, she poured an extra cup of tea and handed it to Rena.

Rena didn't want any tea, until she smelled the warm steam — honey notes. She took it from her grandmother and drank it.

Resuming her seat, Genma sat in the rocker. "Lastly, it is not a thing. It is a bear. Your bear, our bears, are a part of our makeup and soul."

Duly admonished, Rena felt as if she should apologize to her bear for her derogatory remark.

However, the voice rested inside of her, in peace. Rena figured it must have understood she was just trying to sort things out in her head.

Taking another drink of the tea, Rena said, "The sweetener in cured tea and muffins was always honey."

"Yes," Genma lifted her own cup and calmly brought it to her mouth. "For us Were-bears, it is always the honey."

"Wouldn't it just have been easier to tell me?" she accused.

Lifting a brow at her, Genma issued a question of her own. "What would you have said if I'd have brought one of my jars of honey out and handed you a drizzler dripping and said here, Rena, have some."

"I would have said no thank you and turned it down." It was how her mother had trained her.

'Be polite Rena, but don't ever consume it. It will make you sick.' Lillian's voice echoed in her head.

"Exactly. Do you know how hard it was those times in the summer when your mother would bring you for a week at a time and order me not to give certain things to yo-u-u?" Her grandmother's voice broke, and tears welled up in her eyes. It was only the second time in her life she'd seen her grandmother cry.

The first was when her mother dragged her out of her grandmother's house when Rena was thirteen.

"Why did she do it, Grandma? Keep such a secret from me?" Rena stared down into her golden tea, cupping her hand around it to let the warmth seep into her body.

"That story is not mine to tell. She is your mother and even when I don't agree with her I have to respect her decision." Emotions under control again, Genma drank her tea.

Raising her gaze to her, Rena said, "Yet, you brought me here and fed me not only honey but salmon against her wishes."

The corner of her grandmother's mouth twitched with the beginnings of a smile. "Figured out the broth for my vegetable stew did you?"

"Oh, boy did I." A small giggle slipped out of her mouth as she recalled practically licking the bowl at the diner.

"Well, to answer your question. I had to."

Draining her cup, Rena set it on the table. "Why now? You could have done it any time after I left my mother's house."

Her grandmother's dark gaze held hers. "Because not having it was starting to kill you. I couldn't have that."

Rena gasped at hearing the weighted words. Her mind flashed back through the last year, the pain and weakness. The maddening cravings, her bear had been attempting to save its life, save Rena's life. "The illness."

"The illness." Her grandmother declared.

Emotions bombarded her heart and swelled inside her until Rena felt as if she couldn't breathe. Popping up from the couch, she raced to the patio doors. After opening them, she rushed out. Standing at the rail she took in large gulps of air.

Quietly, her grandmother came up beside her and placed a hand at the center of her back.

Staring beyond the woods to the path that led to the lake, Rena said, "Do you think that my mother knew not giving me the honey would kill me?"

"It is doubtful." After giving her back a pat, Genma

pulled her hand away. "Lillian is a full Were-bear. She was raised to understand the power of the honey. Its specific antioxidants we need like most human's need vitamin A, B, C, D and iron. Honey for us does all of those things. I think she believed your human side would just take over fully and if she didn't give you the one thing your bear needed, you would never shift."

Leaning her hips against the rail, she looked at her grandmother. "Grandma, that just doesn't make any sense. Being here in Den I haven't seen anything that would be a deterrent that would make my mom not want me to embrace my shifter side."

Shaking her head, Genma exhaled loud and said, "Your mother is fighting her own ghosts."

Rena felt as if they were getting to the true heart of the matter. "What happened the last time we were here?"

Turning, her grandmother stared at her. "What do you remember?"

Inhaling, Rena thought about all the memories that had unfolded in her mind form the time she had awakened. It was as if everything that had been trapped behind a wall of confusion and uncertainties had been freed. "Everything. But I still don't know why my mother became angry with you, with Den."

Nodding, her grandmother grabbed the railing and hoisted herself over and to the ground.

Even though Rena now knew that her grandmother's strength and agility came from her bear, it would still take her a while not to be shocked by it. Following suit, Rena landed two feet away.

With a twinkle in her eye, her grandmother started down the path toward the lake. "Let me tell you a story."

Keeping pace with her, Rena listened.

"Attraction and love have a way of blossoming naturally in the smallest amount of time. However, for Weres we are drawn in by scents, markings of other shifters. There was once a little girl who came for short visits to see her grandmother. This girl enjoyed her time in the woods and water, under her mother's protection only. Soon the girl made friends and one year met with them at the lake and played for hours. However, every time this child came back she was a little older. The final time she visited her grandmother she was beginning to mature and her scent was now a draw to the boys."

Rena didn't have difficulty following her grandmother's words. She knew Genma was painting a picture of her life. That last summer.

"Weres may be attracted to others of the opposite gender, but only one can be their true mate."

During the days Rena had been in Den County she'd come to realize several things, one being the golden eye color that happened when someone's desire was engaged. She and Genma now stood at the end of the dock overlooking the water. "Cord kissed me that day."

"Greater than that. I don't think she would have taken you away if it wasn't for the fact that his eyes had become golden."

Her brow drew tight as she looked at her grandmother. "But, that's just desire."

"No that is the mating lust. It is only shown for one's life mate."

The full understanding of what her mother had done when she took her away was a stab into Rena's heart. The knowledge angered her. She wanted to scream, kick and claw at something or someone. Her bear was roaring inside of her. Rena's body was tight. "I think it's time you take me to town, Grandma."

"I sure will."

They turned back to the house.

"That painting you did for Cord, could you add two bears on the dock?"

Hugging her waist, her grandmother said, "I thought you'd never ask."

~YH~

"Hello, Cord."

He lay on one of the loungers outside on his stone porch. The same spot he'd been in since getting home yesterday. Looking over at the statuesque blonde woman walking toward him, he said, "Nana."

"How are you?" Coming to him, she placed a kiss on the top of his head as she had done since he was small.

"How's Rena?" he countered. *He* had not just discovered that his whole life was a lie. If his grandmother was here, what did that mean?

She sat on the second lounger. "When I left she had finally awakened. She looked healthy, restored but the strains of uncertainty were evident in her features."

Nodding, Cord sat up and swung his body to the side so he was facing her directly. "That's good to hear. Will Genma tell her the truth?"

"The parts that are hers to tell, she will." Reaching out, his grandmother laid her hand on his knee.

Looking at the woman who'd been a constant strength for him in his life, he had a few questions for her. He was starting to realize that maybe she had not been forthright with him. "Where have you been these last few days? This mystery trip you and Genma had to take."

Crossing her legs, she linked hands around the top of her knee. "Right here in Den."

He frowned. "Where? Someone would have said if they'd seen you and Genma."

"We were at the old starter home. A few miles through the woods beyond Genma's cabin."

For a moment, Cord wasn't sure what place his grandmother was referring too. But, then he recalled that as a young Were, he and his friends would venture deep into the forest. They located the only residence still standing from the time when his great-grandfather had led them here and established a society, a way of life that would protect them. He and his friends used the rundown place as a fort. "That place isn't safe, Nana. How did you two last days in it?"

"Oh, dear, Genma and I have been planning this for months. We contracted Theo to do some work on it, restore it for our stay. We just didn't know when we would use it."

"What?" He eyed the beautiful, secretive woman before him. "I think it's time you really tell me what is going on."

"That's why I'm here."

"Can I assume that whatever you have to say has to do a lot with why Rena was brought here, now?"

"That as well as why Genma contracted you to do the yard work during the no work time in Den."

"Why?" Then something Marcella said to him came to mind. "You wanted us alone at the cabin?"

"Away from distraction is how we thought about it."

He rubbed a hand across his chin, covered with two day's growth of stubble. "All the subterfuge, Nana." He got up from the chair, stalked to the edge of the flagstone patio and stared down at the grass one step away. "Why?"

The chair creaked behind him, moments before his grandmother placed a hand on his shoulder.

"I was there, Cord. The day Lillian took Rena away."

That memory still brought a knot to his stomach. He stood silent.

"Genma radioed me that night after they were gone. My best friend was hurt by her daughter's actions. I rushed over, but Genma didn't want me there for her."

He glanced into the caring eyes of his grandmother, then he had to look away knowing that she could see the pain in his soul.

"When she took me to the dock, I saw you, my Cordy-bear. You were curled up into a tight ball. You had shifted and just sat there, unresponsive to anyone. Your friends or Genma."

"But you," he whispered. Even now the ache of that day, his bear knowing that his life mate had been located and had been ripped away without care or explanation.

She leaned her head onto his shoulder. "Only because I had the idea to shift and got your bear to follow my lead back to your parents' cabin. But, you didn't shift back for almost a week and you refused to eat or drink anything."

Wrapping an arm around his grandmother, he pulled her along his side. "And still you stayed right there with me."

Stretching up on her toes, she kissed his cheek. "I'm

Nana, where was I supposed to be."

He smiled.

She returned his smile then her expression became serious as she said, "Taking Rena away wasn't Lillian's only crime. Genma and I brought Rena here because not acknowledging her bear was killing her. We had to do something."

Dropping his head, Cord struggled to breathe. It had been worse than he suspected. "How could this happen?"

"Lillian told Rena that Den was a horrible place, warned her off from coming here. She'd been lying to Rena since she was a baby that she was allergic to honey and fish...particularly salmon. She raised her child as a vegan. Genma had lost her own daughter and didn't want to cause conflict between Rena and Lillian. When Rena's father passed away the next year, it just got more complicated."

Cord shook his head. That was the most bizarre thing he had ever heard. A bear staying away from things they needed most. "Lillian wouldn't have been able to keep herself away from honey or she'd be dead."

"Very true." His grandmother stepped away and moved back to her lounger. "We couldn't do anything about Lillian. But, when Rena's illness was getting worse we knew we had to do something for her. For me there was my grandson to consider."

Facing her, he wondered how he played a factor in trying to heal Rena. "What about me?"

"I've watched you over the years. Present but not really here in heart. I know the pressure your father has you under with the mayor position having to be filled soon."

"No worries there, Nana, I'm taking it." Cord sat again.

"Oh, sweetheart, I know you are. Besides I heard about that match with Tim from your grandfather." She growled and pretended to make jabs in the air.

Laughter erupted out of him. "It was wrestling, Nana, not boxing."

Lowering her hands, she placed them on her hips. "I know that, but I didn't think you wanted me to get up and throw you to the ground as an example. I was saving your male pride from being lost in the dirt like your cousin's." She winked at him.

He chuckled. "Thanks."

"You're welcome." Sobering she said, "Your great-grandfather, your grandfather and your father have all been blessed with having their true mate at their side as they led this town. I wasn't going to have my grandson doing it with less. If I had anything to do with it. Especially not with that hot-furred Marcella."

Reaching across the space, he took hold of her hand. "What would I do without you?"

"Thank the Great Spirit I'm a Were-bear so it will be many years before you have to find out."

Squeezing her hand, he asked, "What should I do now? I'm torn."

Patting the back of his hand, still holding hers, she said, "You wait. You've had patience all these years. A little more time will not make much of a difference. Let Rena come to you."

That was the opposite of what he wanted to do. He'd be fighting, getting in his truck and driving to Genma's and carrying Rena out of there to his house. Their home. That's what his bear wanted him to do and he was of the same heart and mind.

Staring down at their hands then, he raised his eyes to meet hers. "What if she decides all this is too much and she heads back to her life.

"We'll sort that out when and if the need arises. If we have to hog tie her to a chair, we will." She slapped her thigh.

He knew this feisty old woman and her cohort would. "I'm sure you would."

"Whatever it takes to make sure she gets her last two marks and can't leave you." She pulled her hand away and stood. "Don't think I didn't smell your scent all over her. Now, how about you make your Nana some lunch."

Cord stood as well and led the way into his house. "By the way, there's just the final mark." He pulled the door open.

Pausing she looked at him. "I only saw the one on her shoulder. Do I want to ask where the other one is?"

Holding up his hand, he showed her the healed cut on his finger. "She marked me."

"That's one smart sow." She wagged her finger at him as she went by into the kitchen.

He agreed with his grandmother's assessment of his mate. He wondered if Rena's intelligence would lead her to choose him.

CHAPTER ELEVEN

"Hello, mom." Rena held the phone to her ear. Her grandmother was waiting in the front office talking to Sheriff Smokey.

"Rena? Dear, where have you been? I've been trying to reach you for days now." Her mother said.

"I'm in Den County. I thought you would have recognized the only number in town." Rena paced the floor around the table the phone sat on in the corner. The radio, the main communication method, crackled with conversation going on around the county.

"What are you doing there?" Her mother's voice was tight as if she were speaking through clenched teeth.

Rena could believe her mother was gritting her teeth, because Lillian Hoodman didn't take disobedience well. "No disrespect, but I'm the one who needs questions answered."

"Come home then. When you get to my house I'll explain anything you want to know."

"I have one better for you, mom. You have until this evening to get here or I'll tell Grandma you said she can tell me the truth," she countered.

"Why would you believe someone else's lies?" Her mother ranted. "Don't believe them. Don't eat anything."

"This evening." Rena tuned out Lillian's dogged attempt to still cover her tracks. "At the sheriff's office," she demanded.

"Rena, liste—"

Rena did something she'd never done before, hung up on her mother. Taking a moment, she inhaled a deep breath. She wasn't sure if she'd done the right thing. Even though she wanted answers maybe she should have flown to Adams Town and confronted her mother there.

Her bear whined at the thought. Rena understood clearly the message. It was no longer her destiny to leave Den. The life she'd once known was gone.

However, before she could move forward to her future she had to clean out the cobwebs from her past.

Opening her eyes, she left the back office.

Her grandmother glanced in her direction when Rena opened the door. "Did you talk to her?"

"Yup." Rena walked to the seat beside her grandmother.

Sheriff Smokey stood quietly leaning his shoulder against the wall.

"What did she say?" her grandmother asked.

"Not much once I told her I wasn't talking to her unless she came here to Den."

Genma patted Rena's leg. "Good for you. Oh, to have been a bird on Lillian's windowsill and seen her reaction."

Rena knew how her mother looked when the topic of Den County came into the conversation. It had only taken Rena one time after she'd graduated from high school and she wanted to spend the summer with her grandmother before she left for college. Lillian Hoodman had gone ballistic. Stomping around the house, lecturing and fuming about honor and a daughter's responsibility to honor the wishes of her mother.

It would have been foolish of Rena to point out how her mother was not honoring her own mother by keeping her grandchild away from her. She learned to keep her peace. Over the years, Rena had wondered how her father, a patient and scholarly man, had dealt with her mother's tantrums. Her mother had a tendency to be controlling and self-centered, wanting things her way or no way.

After her father's death, her mother had focused every ounce of her energy on Rena. The reason that after she had completed college she took the first job away from her mother she could find.

"What do you want to do in the meantime?"

"If she comes." Rena fell back onto the wall behind the bench.

"Oh, she will, Red. She will not be able to resist."

Standing, Rena said, "How about we grab food at Gobi's."

Genma stood and smiled. "Sounds like a plan." Heading toward the door, she paused and looked over her shoulder at the stoic lawman. "You care to join us, Sheriff?"

He pushed away from the wall with a look of concern on his face. Rena wondered if he believed her inviting her mother back to Den was going to cause a lot of upheaval in his orderly town.

"No, I need to make the rounds at the grounds. I'll see you two back here later." He followed them out.

"Would you like us to bring you something back? Rolls with homemade sweet butter?"

He gave her a small smile. "Not necessary. I'll grab some delicious treats from one of the booths." Waving them off, he turned and headed across the street toward the festival.

Linking her arm through her grandmother's she asked, "Do you think the sheriff is acting odd?"

"It's a day away from Bear Run, every single male and female bear is behaving out of sorts." Her grandmother chuckled as they continued on to the diner.

Smiling for the first time all day, Rena said, "Bear Run? Hmm, I think I just discovered what we shall talk about over food."

"Which is perfect because that will lead into the discussion of marking...like the one on your shoulder."

~YH~

"See, what did I tell you, Rena? Your mother wouldn't have to worry about the town barriers. Lillian would remember how to find her way in."

Anger contorted her mother's face as she raced across the sheriff's front office toward Genma with an accusing finger aimed at her. "You! I should have known you were behin—"

Genma's growl was low, but piercing.

"No, Mother, I'm the one you'll need to be talking to." Rena rose from Stacey's empty chair behind the desk and approached her mother. She'd never seen the beautiful woman appear so frazzled. Rena could imagine the last minute plane ride from Massachusetts to California. Her mother's black hair was normally perfectly twisted into a bun at the top of her head. Today it was wild and floating like an ebony cloud around her shoulders.

Staring from Genma to her, Lillian said, "Rena, we need to talk—"

Calm and in control, just as her mother had taught her, Rena stood before her. "Yes, we do."

"Not, here." She glanced around, seeing the sheriff and then looked back at Rena. Holding her arms out at her side, Lillian said, "See I've come, just as demanded. Now let's go home."

"But, this place is perfect, Mother, for you to answer for your crimes."

Folding her arms over her chest, Lillian asked, "What supposed crimes have I committed? Being a good mother? I was a single parent for most of your life and raised you to be a bright, well-adjusted young lady." She shot another look at Genma. "Until now."

Rena guffawed. "Attempted murder."

Lillian's head whipped back around, pinning her with a stare. "Really, Rena, such theatrics? You should know better than this."

"I would have thought the same of you. But I was so wrong," Genma said.

Stalking to the bench, Lillian dropped onto it. "See, this is why I kept you from her. I knew they would one day poison your mind against me. Without giving me a chance to defend."

Genma stepped before her daughter, and stared down at her. "You have always been a selfish and willful child. Always having to have things your way or you leave without considering the ramifications of such actions."

Slapping a hand against her chest, Lillian cried, "Rena was my child. Mine to deal with how I saw fit. Underestimating you was the only consequence to my actions."

"What about your father?" Genma's voice lowered. "Your father had gone out to search for you. He wanted to bring you home. But way beyond our territory he'd been killed by a hunter."

For a moment Rena witnessed her grandmother appearing to become the elderly woman her human age indicated. It concerned her. Her grandmother always seemed so strong, invincible. But, Rena realized that the old woman had been carrying around too much hurt and pain, too many secrets.

Stepping to her, Rena wrapped her arms around her grandmother. She leaned against her.

"That wasn't my fault. I didn't know he would look for me. I…I just needed to get away." Lillian's voice no longer held the condescending tone as before, it had become hollow and broken.

Her grandmother sniffed. "He loved you. We loved you. Of course we would have searched for you."

Her mother glanced away, staring at the front door as if she wanted to flee with the same haste as she'd entered the office.

The room grew silent.

Glancing over at the sheriff, whose face was a blank mask but whose onyx eyes were swimming with hidden emotions, Rena found herself choked up by the revelations she had heard. She could imagine this big bear of a man felt something too, even as a bystander. "Sherriff Smokey, can you please take my Grandma into your office?"

With a sharp nod, he said, "I will." Moving to Genma, he slipped a careful arm around her grandmother.

Rena watched as he led her away.

Stopping at the door, Genma looked around his broad shoulder. "It's time for the truth, Lillian. No more secrets."

Her mother didn't respond to her grandmother's words.

She waited until the door was secure before she turned back to her mother. At the moment, with her grandmother in a fragile state and her mother pouting in the seat, Rena felt like the only mature one in the place.

Taking the few steps to reach her mother, Rena sat beside her, not touching, just sitting there. She allowed the silence to stretch as she waited to see if her mother would speak first.

Giving up, Rena began, "Waking up and finding yourself trapped and looking out through the eyes of a bear does something to a woman."

Two beats later, her mother gazed over at her. However, she was still quiet.

"I was so afraid. I didn't know what was happening to me." Rena became choked up recalling that morning and seeing Cord shift from a bear to a man and back to a bear as he followed her through the woods. "Then when I found out that I was a Were, some kind of bear-shifter and no one had told me, because you didn't want them to. I became angry and for a moment I hated you, mother."

Her mother gasped. "Rena, I wasn't trying to—"

"Please don't speak..." Rena let out a ragged breath. "Unless you're prepared to tell me the truth, don't say a damn word."

Crossing her arms, her mother turned her back to her. "I will not sit here and take —"

Rena's head bobbed up and down. "Oh, yes you will. You will sit and you will listen, because you almost ruined my life...kept me from the man I am supposed to be with...almost killed me. Why?" Too many emotions were toppling over inside of her for her to hold back the scream that erupted out of her with that one question. *Why?*

Her mother stood slowly and walked away. Rena thought she would keep walking out the door, never to be heard from again. But, her mother stopped in the center of the room, not looking at her.

Watching her shoulders rise slightly as Lillian took several deep breaths, Rena waited.

"Weres of this town raise their cub-children with fanciful stories about love and being with one's true mate. They teach us that being someone's life mate makes them strong. That two people become one soul, sharing dreams and thoughts and babies. Filling our heads with the notion that there is no greater love." Her mother turned and faced her, her face wet with tears, her eyes empty and lost. "But they don't tell you how to find them, just that you will know when you do."

Her lips curled back in a sneer. "Well, I thought I had. There was a guy who was my friend, but I fell for him hard. Made a fool of myself trying to prove to him we should be together." The chuckle that came out was humorless. "My mother kept telling me to let it go. 'You just can't force these things, Lillian' she would say. So, I stepped back."

Breaking eye contact, her mother looked away

toward the sealed door of the back office then said, "Jasper was a few years older than me. He'd gone away for a while to search out the world, become a more independent man and stronger Were-bear. Mom told me to let him go, that it was possible he wasn't meant for me, but I knew she was wrong. Two years later, the year I graduated, he returned. As soon as I learned he was back, I drove over in the new car my parents had given me. I wanted to impress him with the woman I'd become." She gazed down at the floor. "When I got there it became real clear that he wanted someone else. I saw Jasper kissing Charlotte Ruxpin, the mechanic's daughter. Not just kissing. His teeth were sunk in her wrist, marking her. I screamed and when they glanced over at me both their eyes were golden. I just reacted. Went home and packed. When my parents tried to tell me to take some time, that there was a Were for me, I waited until they were asleep and left." Glancing over at her, Lillian said, "All I could think about was the same thing happening to you. Those Bjorn men, as well as all the other men in Den, can't be trusted not to play with a woman's heart."

Rena shook her head at her mother's words. Her own experience in town had been completely opposite. "Did dad know before he died?"

"No. It was too unsafe." Her mother shook her head and sighed. "I ended up in West Virginia and enrolled in a local college. All those trees and mountains allowed me space to roam when I needed to. After I found out what happened to my dad, not knowing he was looking for me when it happened. I knew I wasn't ready to return to Den." In front of her again, Lillian said, "You have to believe me when I say I didn't know my father went looking for me the weeks following my leave."

Holding the sad gaze of her mother, Rena did believe her. With all of the things her mother may have done, it was evident in her voice that she loved her father.

"I do believe you. But why didn't you ever come back before I was born?"

"I was still hurt and licking my wounds." Exhaling, her mother sat beside her again. "Larry was one of the professors at the college. A kind older man who wanted someone to care for and I needed to be cared for." She shrugged. "It worked for us."

Rena thought of her father, a sweet absentminded professor type. He'd loved them both up until he had a heart attack at work. She missed him. Soon after his death, her mother moved them to the small town of Adams, Massachusetts, by Mount Greylock and Rena now understood why. They began to visit Den County for a week in the summers.

"Then when you were born, I knew there was a chance you wouldn't have the gene. I hoped that you would be full human."

"You raised me with fears of foods? You restricted my diet—"

"Just to make sure." Her mother placed a hand on her leg then removed it as if she was unsure if Rena wanted a connection with her. "If I'd known the gene was latent or that your sickness was due to your bear trying to fuse with you..." This time she touched her shoulder and didn't move her hand as she stared into Rena's eyes. "I would have never done it."

Giving her a small smile, she said, "I believe you." She did. Her mother may be a lot of things but evil wasn't it.

Sighing loudly, her mother leaned back against the bench.

"There's just one last thing I need to know, Mom." Rena kept her eyes trained on her mother.

"What is that?" she asked, cautious. "I thought I answered everything."

"Not quite. What happened the last day we were here? What was the argument with grandmother about?"

"I had enjoyed each summer with Grandma. Then in an instant it was all gone and you wouldn't even let me talk about it."

"I know you did like coming here. You hadn't shown any Were traits, so I thought it was fine to bring you here and I would keep a sharp eye out, protect you. However, I guess I didn't keep you sheltered enough because Jasper's son still got to you."

Now that Rena understood, thanks to her grandmother, more about being a bear shifter and how they are led to their mates, she knew that Cord hadn't 'got to her' he'd been drawn to her. Unable to stop that kiss if he'd wanted to. But Rena held her tongue, it was evident that her mother had never known that bonding kind of love.

"Anyway, I got angry when your grandmother said that it was possible that the Great Spirit didn't place me with Jasper because he had plans for his son and my daughter." Lillian huffed and rolled her eyes.

"That part is true mother. Very true." Rena held her mother's gaze, black as night, evidence that Lillian belonged to Den County, even if she didn't want to admit it. "Cord is my mate. Even then, with my gene being suppressed he still found me."

Placing a hand on her arm, her mother said, "I just

hope you're right. I want you to be happy. That was all I ever wanted." Leaning into Rena, she embraced her.

Rena couldn't hold back the tears that fell from her eyes. This was all she'd ever wanted from her mother. To have her understand and accept that Rena was her own person, able to make decisions for herself without all the subterfuge and control.

They heard the door open to the back office. Turning, they saw her grandmother walking out first. A few steps away, Genma gazed down at her daughter. It shocked Rena to see the uncertainty on her grandmother's face. The older woman had always been so strong and confident since Rena had known her, now she looked unsure.

Moving away from Rena, her mother rose and took a step closer to her grandmother. "Mom, I'm so sorry. I didn't know that dad would follow me. I just wanted to get away."

Closing the gap, Genma wrapped her arms around her daughter. Hugging her, Genma said, "He loved you so much. We both did. All we ever wanted was the best for you, for you to find your mate."

Rising from the bench, Rena's heart swelled as she saw the two most important women in her life finally coming together and healing the past.

Kissing her mother on the cheek, leaning back she said, "I was very content, Mom, with Larry. I don't think the Great Spirit has a mate for me —"

"You were always looking in the wrong direction." Sheriff Smokey's voice rumbled deep and brought the conversation to a halt.

All three women turned and faced the only man in the room. Up until this point the lawman had been a silent observer who was willing to stand back and let the females handle their family issues. Rena was beginning to believe she'd perceived the big guy's actions all wrong.

"That was apparent and the reason I left," Lillian said.

He pushed away from the wall, where he'd been leaning since he escorted her grandmother back into the room. Moving closer to her mother, he continued. "Did you ever think, Lillian Berend, that maybe the day you hightailed your sweet ass out of Den that you snatched away the possibility for you to find your mate and his opportunity to declare himself to you?"

Her mother lifted a shoulder, saying, "Who knows, the past is the past. I'm Hoodman, now."

Rena watched the big bear of a man strut across the room, slow and purposeful. He stopped directly in front of her mother. "It should have been Smokey."

The shocked gasp coming from her mother's mouth ‚was the perfect sound to Rena's own response. With wide eyes she stared at the couple before her. Her grandmother stepped back beside Rena, a knowing smile on her lips.

"What are you saying, David?" Using his given name, something Rena hadn't heard anyone do since she'd been in the county. She noted how transfixed her mother's gaze was on the sheriff's face, seeming to search it for the truth in his words.

"You're not getting away from me again. I plan to make you mine as I'd planned to do the day after our graduation." His hand reached up, cupping Lillian's face. "Don't make me live without you again."

Rena didn't expect her mother's reaction.

Stretching up on her toes, Lillian kissed him. When they parted, Rena heard her mother sigh and the low growl coming from the male Were, accompanied by the flecks of gold revealed in both of their ebony eyes.

Smiling at the pair, Rena heard her grandmother say, "My job here is done."

Laughing, Rena didn't even try to figure out what her grandmother had been ferreting out of the lawman while they had been in the back office. With her mother in town and the sheriff declaring his intentions, things in Den had just gotten very interesting.

~YH~

"If you two are on my doorstep it can't be good." Cord stared at the ladies on his porch.

"Oh, come on now, Cordy-bear. Why can't a grandmother decide to have lunch with her grandson?" His grandmother gave him one of her sweet, innocent grins as she stepped to him and kissed his cheek, then breezed by him into his cabin.

"Oh, course you can, Nana." He eyed her strutting directly to his long couch and taking up residence.

"We thought you could use a little company." Genma, his grandmother's cohort's smile was just a matronly as she brushed her lips across his other cheek and followed her friend in and claimed the seat beside her.

Shaking his head, Cord was even more convinced these two were up to something. Sweet they both were, but too elderly to be plotting something, absolutely not. Closing his door, he turned back to his living room to see what he could glean from his visitors. He cared for both of them. However, after two days of not seeing or hearing from Rena he was hoping she was the one knocking at his door. Too many times to count he'd grabbed the keys for his truck and started for Genma's or stood in front of his radio ready to channel up the

Berend house to just hear her voice. But his grandmother had told him to give her some time and that she had a lot of adjustments going on.

He knew his Nana was right. Rena's mother was back in town and rumors were going on and on about the three ladies, Rena, Genma and Lillian spending time together and getting along. Den residents were saying that Lillian was a completely different person than she had been before she left town. Cord wondered how much Lillian's change of heart had to do with the large bear of a sheriff courting her. He wanted to do the same thing with Rena, but his grandmother had said he needed to let her come to him, be patient. So he waited.

"How can I help you ladies?" Standing in the center of his living room, with his thumbs hooked in his pockets, he stared at them looking all too comfortable on his couch.

"Genma and I were out and about today and thought we'd come over for lunch," Octavia said.

"Lunch?" The word fell out of his mouth as he frowned at them. This was not what he'd expected they were here for. "How's Rena?"

"Oh, there is plenty of time to discuss things later... what are we having?"

Pressing his tongue hard to the roof of his mouth and gritting his teeth, he stifled the growl his bear was trying to let out. They were in one accord when it came to wanting information on their mate, if they couldn't see her. He exhaled. He knew that these two ladies wouldn't give away any secret until they were ready. There was no need for him to do anything but play along.

"How does seared tuna and grilled honey-glazed

peaches sound?" He asked.

"Oh, I love tuna with a nice garden salad." His grandmother said.

"With the perfect glass of sweet iced tea will just bring out the flavor of those peaches," Genma volunteered.

Glancing at each other as if he wasn't even the one that was preparing it, they filled out the rest of his menu. Folding his arms, he stood silently until they decided they needed something from him.

His grandmother looked to him first. "That just sounds delicious. Can't wait to eat."

Guess that means get to it, he surmised. "Coming right up. Give me a few minutes." Chuckling, he headed in the direction of his kitchen.

After he'd taken a few steps he heard Genma say, "Tea, Cord, some warm tea while we wait for lunch would be wonderful."

"Do you still have some of Genma's muffins, a plate of that would hit the spot and tide us over until lunch is ready," his nana added.

He paused and smiled over his shoulder, ever the obedient grandson. "I'll have them both right out for you two."

They rose, simultaneously, as if joined at the hips.

"Oh, bring them to the kitchen table, we can chat and nibble while lunch is being prepared," his grandmother instructed.

"That's an excellent idea, Octavia," Genma cheered as they beat a trail past him into his kitchen first.

Great Spirit help me, this is going to be a long afternoon.

Forty-minutes later, they were all seated at the table with steaming plates of tuna and peaches, a fresh seasonal salad and chilled glasses of honey-sweetened iced tea. It had only taken him a few minutes to realize earlier that when the two grandmothers had stated they all would chat while he cooked, what they meant was the two of them would pretend his cabin was some sort of café where they would talk about everything under the sun, but Rena. The one conversation he'd been hoping for.

"Can I get anything else for you ladies?" Cord glanced at his grandmother first, then Genma.

"No, we are fine. So ready to eat." Nana smiled at him.

"I'm famished. Can't wait to dig in," Genma said.

Cord nodded sharply, then picked up his fork.

"Oh, here you are, Cord," Genma pulled a small envelope out of her purse and slid it across the table to him. "Rena told me to give you this." Her dark gaze was innocent, as if she and his grandmother didn't know he would have wanted them at his door with this held out to him instead of having him go through so much 'singing and dancing'.

Frustrated, the low growl slipped out before he could catch it.

"Oh, is that your stomach. You must be hungry, too." Genma started eating.

"You must try the peaches, Genma. They are sweet and tender," Octavia encouraged, seemingly oblivious to the male Were at the table.

Ignoring them, he raised the letter to his nose. He allowed his bear's sense to cipher through all the unimportant scents on it, like Genma's woodsy herbal notes and the smell of mint that most likely came from peppermints in her purse. Finally, he located and pulled forth the one he was looking for, honeyed asters: floral, sweet and intoxicating. That was his

Rena.

My mate. His bear roared in satisfaction.

Smelling the small trace of her scent wasn't as good as having her before him, by any stretch, but it was all he had at the moment. He'd gratefully take it. Two days without her was too long.

He lowered it then slipped the small card out from inside. It read:

CORD,

I HOPE TO SEE YOU AT THE DANCE THIS EVENING.

~YOURS RENA

Cord started to rise from his seat, he was ready to go to her now. The warm hand on his left arm was his grandmother's stilling him from his departure. His mind and his bear on one thing, getting to Rena, he'd practically forgotten the two partners in crime were even there.

Stunned, he stared down at her strong, elegant fingers that held his arm. "No need to rush off in haste. There's plenty of time for you to finish your lunch."

"The tuna is flakey and divine, you must try some. A hungry bear is an impatient bear." Genma winked at him.

Cord knew they were both right. The dance wouldn't even begin for a couple hours. There was no need for him to go racing into town and scare all the cubs as he paced up and down the street waiting for her. Relaxing in his seat, he began eating, since the two grandmothers weren't planning to let him leave the table until he'd finished.

Feeling his own hunger, he picked up his fork again and dug in.

"Cord, I don't think I've had a chance to thank you

for everything you did at my house..." her voice drifting away, Genma paused.

Raising his gaze to meet her, he saw the warmth and true meaning in her dark eyes. In a way, he knew that even though Genma and his grandmother had orchestrated the entire event with him and Rena, his grandmother's best friend saw him as a strong, protective...worthy male. That, made him feel honored. She appreciated him looking out for her property, more importantly claiming her granddaughter. As Weres, everything came down to that one responsibility—claiming. Everything else came from that instinct. And he'd see it through.

"You're welcome."

"Oh, that yard did turn out lovely," his grandmother chimed in, as if she wasn't aware of the deeper, emotional, silent conversation at the table.

Turning to her, Genma chattered on, high-spirited. "Didn't it. The soil of my garden is tilled and ripe for planting. Lillian has been helping me get everything organized. Next week we will start getting the seeds in the ground."

"Oh, that Lillian always did have one hell of a green paw." Octavia picked up her sweating glass of tea and drank.

"Yes, yes, she does. I do believe my vegetables will have an added sweetness to them when they sprout."

He ate, and tried to keep his patience as the two grands carried on the conversation around the table. His body may be present with them, but his mind, heart, soul and bear were all focused on Rena. His mate.

Mine. Claim her.

That's exactly what he planned to do tonight.

CHAPTER TWELVE

Leaning up against the Grand Grizzly Arcade in the center of town, Cord scanned the crowd as he'd been doing the last two hours since he'd arrived at the dance. The main street that ran through town was packed. All Weres in the county were present and moving to the music along the street. This was the first year the planning committee had decided to throw a dance before the Bear Run and it was a success. Outside of the fathers dancing with their daughters or the mothers trying not to have their toes stepped on by awkward young males, it was a lusty, flirting frenzy. Unmated mature Weres sniffing around each other like someone was hiding a honey pot. The females were beguiling in their sultry moves and the males were practically drooling from their mouths.

However, none of that mattered to Cord. The only thing he waited on was Rena to arrive. The dance was almost over and his heart had been racing with apprehension that maybe she had changed her mind and decided she didn't want this life, or him. That's the part that gnawed deeply at his stomach. It dug into his gut and made him second guess every action he'd taken with her since he'd kissed her on the dock years ago. This was still all new to her, a lot to ask her to accept about herself and them.

It was the reason his grandmother had instructed him to keep away from her. 'Give Rena some time, Cord. Let her sort this out for herself and come to you. This can't be forced.'

Even though he understood that in his head, his heart was a different matter. And his bear was an entirely different beast. All his bear wanted to do was share with Rena the third and final mark. It was the one that would bind them together. The single mark that would not allow her to leave him, or him her, without it killing the other. A painful death.

She arrived. He knew it the moment she strutted down Paw Tracks Street. His bear had gone on full alert. Cord became aware of the tingling sensation running along his spine causing heat to spiral through his core.

He tracked her progress toward him with his gaze. She was dressed in a passion red tank top that matched the color of the ripe strawberry mark on her hip. A mark he recalled vividly. The air outside was crisp, with a breeze chilled from the overcast sky, but because of their bear trait they maintained high internal temperatures. Rena's sleeveless body-hugging top wasn't any different than the kind of apparel others were dancing around in. The jeans she wore fit her curves and long legs like they had been custom-made around her. Her captivating ebony locks hung in loose waves around her shoulders. He recalled burying his hands in her hair as she took him deep in her mouth, loving the length of his cock, that same part of him that was even now hard and pressing against his jeans.

His bear urged him to go to her, toss her over his shoulder and walk away from the dance with her to the first available spot they found where he could strip her, lay her down and take care of the final mark. Cord agreed wholeheartedly with his bear. The thought of where it was customary to place the mark made his body tremble with need. He could almost taste that area of her skin.

Shoving away from the wall, he met her in the center of the street, gyrating bodies and laughter all around them. But everyone else was blocked out from his mind.

"Hello, Cord." Her voice was low and husky.

"Hi, Red." He enjoyed calling her by that nickname. It brought to mind her birthmark and made his heart race. He gazed into her eyes, noticing that they were still hazel, but instead of the dark brown flecks they were now red—proof of her mixed genes. No onyx eyes for his mate.

"I like the new coloring."

"My grandmother has surmised it is a trait brought out by my birthmark...a bear paw."

Smiling at her, he confessed, "I know." He had enjoyed tracing the details with his tongue.

"I like the new haircut. I'll miss the longer length though."

He rubbed his shorter locks. "I figured it was time I started looking a little more clean-cut like the mayor is supposed to."

She nodded. "You'll do great."

He didn't want to discuss his coming position. He had better things on his mind to do with his time. Grabbing her hand, he said, "Come with—"

"Will you dance with me, Cord?" As alluring as warm honey as she linked her fingers through his.

The simple touch was so slow and sensual it caused his heart to pound hard and his cock to leap. His bear whined from the sublime pleasure. He couldn't deny how much power she had over him and his bear, and they both loved it.

"Yes." Taking the single step, he closed the gap between them as he slipped his arm around her waist. The feel of her body pressed against his caused a humming of deep satisfaction in his soul. This was what he had wanted over the past two days, just to hold her and know she was all right. Female Weres were strong and capable in their own right. However, it was his job to still shelter and protect her. Reasons that Were-males in Den always worked with the builders to have their own cabins and lands built when they had reached maturity and female Were stayed at home under their father's protection until they were mated. A mama bear could rip out a grown male Were's throat in protection of her cubs or mate, but everyone in Den knew the established roles and lived by them happily.

The music shifted from the popular Pop beats to a more rhythmic slow song. Cord didn't care what was played because he was going to hold his mate.

As the clouds in the sky floated overhead, Cord was surrounded by the scent of Rena. Her natural aroma seduced him and drew him closer to her. Lowering his head to her neck, he dragged his nose along the slender column as he inhaled deeply.

"I've missed you." He pressed his lips to her ear and whispered.

She sighed and moved closer, her unrestrained breasts flattening against his chest. "I've missed you too. My soul has ached without you."

Hearing her words, his hand tightened around hers. Leaning back, he gazed into her unique eyes. "Are you okay?"

Rena nodded, understanding what he was asking. "I am. This has been a stressful week but it has all led me to you, now. Where I want to be."

His bear roared, pleased by his mate.

Shifting her hips, she pressed closer to him as she seductively ground her pelvis against his cock.

He growled, allowing the low, deep rumble to vibrate against her chest.

She gasped and her eyes sparkled with metallic threads.

A soft golden haze was beginning to seep in at the peripheral of his vision, he was sure that she could see the color change of his eyes, signifying that his mating lust was triggered and elevating fast. It had been simmering since he'd gotten her short note from Genma. Soon it would be fully engaged and he wouldn't be able to control his actions not to mate with her, wherever and whenever.

Since it was frowned upon to mate out in the open, in undesignated places, as mayor-to-be he couldn't take her in the heart of town.

"Good evening, everyone. This year's First Frost Moon Festival has been a success. Thanks for all the participation in the events, the booths, crafts produced and everything." Jasper's heavy voice rumbled through the microphone.

The crowd cheered, agreeing with the mayor's words.

Rena stopped dancing and turned in his arms to give his father her attention. Cord couldn't care less what the closing speech would entail, all he could think about was his mate. Keeping his arm around her waist he placed a kiss on the curve of her shoulder, making her shiver.

Glancing toward the DJ stand where his father was, Cord saw his mother, Charlotte, standing proudly beside her life mate. Years ago they had been in his same position, claimed each other. They had taken on the position as leaders in their community, birthed three children and continued to share their love openly.

That's what Cord wanted with Rena. Would have with Rena.

"Now that the festival is officially concluded, that only leaves one other event to take place. The Bear Run."

The atmosphere exploded with uproarious roars and clapping. The female Weres gave the men around them seductive looks while the males sniffed the air attempting to detect the scent of their mate. Cord had heard that half the fun of the run was chasing down the strong trace that drew them. Tracking that sensual bouquet was a guarantee that a bear shifter would locate his mate. It was a time-old tradition that had guided countless Weres. Occasionally, because of timing of when a Were chose to participate in the run they could have no success in finding their perfect mate, but would settle for a willing female.

"I will take it by the shouts and roars that everyone is ready. Without delaying this any further, all those unattached mature Were that plan to participate, please make your way to the designated area." As if his father's announcement had been a gunshot starting a race, males and females ran toward vehicles to drive to the clearing on the other end of town only used for the Bear Run.

Unlike all the other unattached Were-bears, Cord didn't need to go on a sniffing adventure.

Taking hold of Rena's hand, he tugged her behind him as he started toward his truck.

Two steps later he felt her resistance. Facing her, he frowned. "What's wrong, sweetheart?"

"Nothing, I am perfectly fine." She still had not started forward.

"Then let's get out of here. I just want to get you home and make love to you." Leaning in, he kissed her lightly on her mouth, he knew if he did any more than that he wouldn't be able to stop.

"I want that too, Cord, but…"

He stared into her eyes, he could see in the color of them that her mating lust was just as elevated as his. "But?"

"I'm going to the Bear Run and I'd like you to join me there."

He chuckled at her naivety. "There's no need. I already know who my mate is. Hell, we both have a mark to prove it." He held his finger up to her.

She smiled and her eyes darkened as she stared at the healed scar. "Yes, but we are going to do this right this time," she declared. "No more accidental bites or ignorance on my behalf. I know who I am, Cord. In the last two days I've become very comfortable with all my changes and connected with my bear." Untangling her fingers from his, she took a step back.

That single action caused an ache in him. His bear whined at the absence of her touch.

"If you want to put that final mark on me, you're going to have to find me to do it." Winking at him, she started to turn but he called out stopping her.

"If this is what you want, Red, I'm willing go. However, I'm going to find you. Make no mistake of that. When I do, you better be ready because I'm going to mark you as mine forever, then I don't plan to stop fucking my life mate until the sun comes up."

He saw the shiver course through her body and the metallic and ruby gaze that met his. She nodded, then without another word headed back down the street the way she had come.

Cord stood rooted to the spot as he watched her walk to her car. There weren't any concerns in Den of safety, but she was his mate and protecting was always top priority.

"That's one bold, she-bear you have there, my cousin." Tim came up beside him.

Not taking his gaze off Rena, Cord said, "Yes she is, just how I like her. Perfect."

"Then if you plan to make sure she's yours, I wouldn't let her get too far ahead of you, Mr. Soon-To-Be Mayor," Tim teased.

Seeing Rena get in her car, Cord faced his cousin who stood with his arm around Nita, his wife. Now that they had battled and Cord's dominance had been proven they were on excellent terms, it was the way of the Were. All hatchets got buried for the good of the community.

"Trust me, I won't." Waving goodbye, Cord hustled toward his truck.

Once he was behind the wheel, he made haste to the

clearing. His mate was headed to the woods with the full-body of her mating pheromones pouring out of her pores. There wasn't any damn way he was going to give another bear a chance to even get a whiff of her. It was true that since he had already marked her and they could share visions during the peak of ecstasy and other males would scent him on her. It was still possible for a male to bite her three times in a row and remove his and Rena's connection. Their creator had made them that way in case a mate was lost. So, two marks between mates didn't ensure anything.

The drive seemed the longest of his life. Three miles down the rocky road outside of town along the path of the river and Cord finally arrived at the designated place. As he pulled into the area he saw cars, people and clothes all over the area. Everyone was preparing to start the run. Generally the males were courteous enough to give the females a head start. But Cord had already seen a couple she-bears take off into the trees and almost instantly be followed by a handful of males.

Finding Rena, happy she made it safely, he parked his truck along-side her grandmother's wagon. When she spotted him, she gave him a delicate finger wave as she stood in only a white pair of lacy thongs, captivating against the deep sienna skin tone. Her beautiful breasts were bare and made his mouth water to lick and taste them all over again. All her other clothing was piled up on top of her car hood.

"Thought maybe you changed your mind," she taunted him, as she hooked her thumbs inside the band of her panties.

"No fucking way. You know we can end this right here?"

"No fucking way." She laughed as she repeating his words. Removing her underwear she sling shot them to him and called out, "See you in the woods, Mr. Bjorn. Catch me if you can."

He caught them, chuckling at her seductive antics. He didn't need her panties to capture her scent, it never left his mind. Flashing her his teeth, incisors and canines lowered in place, he winked at her.

Her eyes flashed with heat as she inhaled, nostrils flaring. She turned toward the forest and he watched her pause for only a moment, as he assumed she was picturing her bear. A few shimmers later she was vaulting through the trees and out of sight.

Shit. Snatching his t-shirt over his head at the same time he was toeing his shoes off, he didn't care if anything was torn or ruined. The only thing he wanted was to get to his mate. Yanking his jeans open, he heard the sounds of the teeth to his zipper strain and snap a second before he had them dropped to the ground. He raced forward, shifting in a tenth of a second. Paws pounding on the ground, he dug into the soil.

Sniffing and running, he eliminated one scent after the other: trees, vegetation, small woodland animals and the other females. Then he isolated on one scent, stronger to him than all the others and he knew he'd locked onto his mate. Rena's scent, as alluring as warm honey.

Her bear called to his, beckoned him to find and claim her. His bear answered the call. Letting out a roar, he knew that wherever she was in the forest she would hear it, sense him. Know he was coming to her, for her.

Cord wasn't concerned that he hadn't spotted her

yet. He knew the woods better than she did. As a new bear, she was going more off sight. He was using straight instinct and her scent. Following that heady trail would clue him into what path she was taking, and where she would end up.

Moving faster, he crashed his big body through bushes on hot pursuit of her. Her smell was so strong now his bear could practically taste it. She was headed to the river. If she made it there and into the water before he caught up with her it would dilute her scent. He wasn't going to let that happen. Taking the straight route to her instead of the winding trail Rena had been following allowed him to cut her off.

Rounding the base of a large redwood, he sprang into the clearing before her.

Rena's bear, unprepared for his appearance before her, slammed in to him. The impact of her animal hitting his in full force caused him to pitch backwards. They toppled over each other once…twice…three times before they landed in a mass of human limbs, both of them having shifted at some point.

Once their bodies were no longer in motion, Cord immediately rolled Rena onto her back. He pressed his body onto hers as he grabbed hold of her hands and pulled them above her head. Laying his mouth on hers, he kissed her. One that wasn't gentle or kind, but demanding of her submission and pleasure. Her breasts were crushed beneath his chest, her tight nipples piercing him. He could feel her heartbeat synchronized perfectly to his.

He slipped his legs in between hers, working them further apart until he could situate himself against her. Never stopping the kiss, he ground his hard, throbbing cock along her sex. Her wet heat coated his shaft.

She moaned.

Yes, he needed to mark her, but he needed to be inside of her just once first.

Of one accord with him, she opened her legs further, allowing him more access as she wrapped her long, toned limbs around his hips.

Pulling his mouth away, he stared into the unique eyes of his woman. The dual blend was something that was special only to Rena, his half-blood bear shifter, and he loved it. It had started raining while he had been chasing her. The water beaded up on her skin and made her scent earthier. He growled, enjoying the mix to her fragrance. "I need you."

"Yes." She licked his bottom lip. "It's been too long, come inside me, love me."

No further encouragement was needed. He released one of her hands and slipped his between their bodies and taking hold of his shaft, he guided himself to her opening. Once there he thrust forward, not stopping until he was seated deep in her core. He made no apologizes for his forcefulness. His need for her was too great for him to be gentle.

Responding to his demand, she buried her heels into the muscles of his ass while she pressed her pussy against him. Her labia surrounding the base of his cock, she took him deeper.

"Don't stop, Cord." She was planting kisses along his nose, jaw and lips as she whimpered. "Please."

Wrapping one arm under her shoulders and the other below her ass, he lifted her higher. Positioning her so that she could receive the full impact of his thrusts, he began to move. Lowering his head, he licked the watery rivers flowing over her skin. He pistoned his hips forward and enjoyed feeling her meeting him each time. She accepted all of him as she called out his name.

Hearing his name on her lips egged him on. He pounded harder into her. Her whimpers and moans of pleasure became a symphony to him.

He needed to feel her come. This wasn't for him. He wanted to take her beyond herself and then feel her unfold beneath him and shower him with her pleasure.

"Come on, babe, I want to taste all that sweet cream. Give it to me, Red." Pushing her hard, he ground his pelvis and brushed along the slick warm walls of her sex.

In response to his actions, she dug her nails deep in his back pulling them along his spine as the wall of her pussy tightened around him and squeezed along his shaft.

"Fuck, that's it, sweetheart. Let go." Arching his back, he brought his head down and nipped at the sensitive tip of a breast.

Crying out, she came. Her body quaked under his, thrashing and bucking. His name became a song on her lips, his heart rejoiced.

Waiting on his own completion, he unwound her legs from around him. Even as her body still quivered, he rose on his knees. With the tips of his fingers, he dragged them slowly down her body and felt her warmth through the sweat and water.

Sighing, she gazed up at him understanding of what was to come evident in her relaxed features. He smiled down at her as he took her breasts in his hands.

Whimpering, she rolled her bottom lip between her teeth and bit down.

Massaging the twin peaks, he loved her instant response to him.

His bear was urging him on with forceful demands to claim her.

The rain had stopped and the First Frost Moon was out now and full, shining brightly between the high tops of the trees.

Grabbing her behind the knees, he pulled her legs high and wide to see all of her. The moonlight beamed down on her sex and illuminated the wetness coating her folds. He growled, wanting to taste every furrow and plain, then suckle her clit.

Before going to the place he desired most, he bent down and placed a kiss on her birthmark. He then dragged his tongue over the crease of her hip joint and followed it down to her pussy. Once there he inhaled deeply and took in the rich ambrosia of her scent—honeyed asters.

His cock throbbed. He wanted to bury it inside her again, but this time that came second to his need to claim her completely. Using the tip of his tongue, he created a path up her slit and around her clit collecting her spicy, sweet essence.

Rena's hands clutched at his shoulders as she lifted and gyrated her hips, chasing after the movements of his tongue.

He understood where she wanted him. His greedy mate was seeking another orgasm. It was apparent in her strong grasp, the arch of her hips and the soft pleading she whispered.

Not distracted from his mission, he caressed the side of her clit, circled it and drew it into his mouth. Flicking it, he brought her to the edge of erotic insanity.

Moving away from her bud of desire, he slipped his tongue inside her, tasting her nectar and drinking deeply of her.

"Cord...Cord, I need —"

Her words broke away as he thrust in and out of her. Grabbing her hips he lifted her from the ground and held her to his mouth.

Moaning she tried again. "Please... Cord, I need to com —"

Removing his tongue from her delectable pussy, he turned his head to the side mere millimeters away. Letting his bears teeth drop, he sank them into the supple flesh of her inner thigh. Claiming his mate and uniting them for life.

Rena came, palming the back of his head, holding him to her as her body thrashed and bucked against his mouth.

As she was still in the throes of her orgasm, he licked her final mark and healed it. He rose above her. "You are *mine*, mate."

Laying her hands on his cheeks, she smiled and responded, "Always and forever."

"I love you, Red." he growled as he kept his gaze on hers and slid his cock into her sex.

"As I love you, my mate." Pulling his mouth down to hers, she kissed him as he made love to her.

EPILOGUE

Rena stood in the center of the fairgrounds on the platform beside Cord, her life mate and husband, before the crowd. It had been a month since the Bear Run and now she was blessed to stand beside him as he took his rightful place in the community.

"Thank you, everyone, for being here today. This has been a moment, long overdue." Jasper, Cord's father, spoke to the residents of Den as he linked his fingers with his wife, Charlotte's, while in his other hand he held the key to the County.

During the month, Cord had traveled to North Carolina with her to end her lease on her apartment and clear out her things. Most of her things went to charity shops that would donate the money for her furniture to battered women's shelters. She was now completely moved into *their* cabin and happy.

As she listened to the current mayor explain the responsibility of the office, she allowed her gaze to travel over the people gathered. Her heart lifted when she saw her mother, Lillian snuggled under the thick arm of the sheriff, looking pleased as a bear in a river during salmon season.

She and Cord had finally emerged from the woods in the morning with the other mated couples and had dressed then drove back into town for the mass joining ceremony. Her surprise was seeing her mother and David as one of the assembled couples. Sherriff David Smokey had made good on his promise then promptly flew with her mother to her house and moved her to Den, for good. It warmed Rena's heart to know that her mother had shaken off all her ghosts of the past and allowed herself to be loved.

Rena even smiled when her gaze skimmed past Marcella, the sow who had been spreading her scent all around Cord in an attempt to have him mark her. The petite Asian beauty was currently snuggled in close to her life mate Rand, the new head manager at Digging Deep Landscaping.

Moving from one face to the next, Rena's gaze paused at her new friend, Greta. Her grandmother's neighbor stood beside her parents. Rena had expected to see Greta emerge from the woods claimed by a male Were, but her friend was nowhere to be found. Apparently, Greta had chosen not to participate. That realization had plagued Rena, but with everything going on, Rena didn't have time to talk with her friend. However, it was on her list to do soon.

"Cord, please come forward." His father called him over to stand beside him.

Rena received the quick kiss Cord gave her before he stepped away. Standing before his father, she admired the bear shifter that was her mate. He was not only tall, imposing and generous both emotionally and physically, he was a strong leader. She had no doubt that he was the perfect person for the job.

"Corduroy Bjorn, my son, I am honored to pass the County Key to you." Jasper held the large wooden key toward Cord. Once Cord took hold of it with two hands, one on each side of his father's, Jasper continued, "The responsibility of Den County and its residents and our way of life was started by your great-grandfather. It passed to his first son, your grandfather, who then passed it to me. Now I give it to you with hopes that at the right time you will hand it to your own first son."

Rena's throat became tight. The emotions of the day were building on her, as well as hearing her father-in-law's words. She and Cord already discovered while they were away last week that she was pregnant. However, they had decided to wait until after the ceremony before sharing the news with anyone. Their secret for now.

"Thanks, Dad. I will use all of the wisdom the Great Spirit gives to lead and govern with truth, honor and fairness. As my strength abounds through the claiming of my mate and any offspring we are blessed to have, I will protect the shifter under my authority."

"I know you will, Son." Jasper let go of the key and pulled Cord into a strong bear-hug.

When the men parted, Cord kissed his mother on her cheek then turned to Rena.

Her heart leaped at the love she saw reflected in his dark gaze.

"Come here, Red." He waved her over to his side. When she was there, he unashamedly kissed her before the crowd.

Everyone applauded, as they shouted their

approval.

When Cord ended the kiss and wrapped his arm around her shoulder, she snuggled close to his side and smiled at everyone gathered.

The moment Cord held the County Key high above his head, the cheers from the sleuth of bear shifters became a roar of excitement. As she observed the pleasure on the faces surrounding them, her gaze landed on Genma and Octavia, their grandmothers.

It took her a moment to figure out what the cohorts were doing, when finally she realized they were rubbing hands over their bellies as they grinned broadly at her and Cord.

As Rena stood there stunned, her life mate pressed his lips to her ear. "I think they know."

"They do. I don't even want to know how they found out," she whispered back.

"It doesn't matter, now. They've probably already orchestrated the design of the baby's room."

Rena laughed at the truth of his words. Her heart was full and she was more than content in her world. She'd come to Den County sick, tired and unsure of what direction her life was going to take next. Now she was stronger than ever, one with her bear, her family was whole and she had more love and support around her than she could've dreamed possible.

Turning to the bear shifter beside her, out of everything that she had gained, he was the best gift of all.

Mine, her bear roared and Rena agreed.

Coming in 2014

*Greta has worked hard at hiding a horrible memory behind her sweet smile, but when a man, she always tried to think of as a brother, comes blazing into Den County turning her life upside down and making her face the past... Greta has to decide if she's woman enough to be **Hansel's Bear**.*

ABOUT THE AUTHOR

I've been penning erotic tales since 2006, on the hedonistic side of the romance genre. However, I've been writing romance under a different pen for a while. I'm eclectic by nature. My stories range from paranormal, contemporary, BDSM, sci-fi and historical. Mostly short stories, but occasional full-length novels.

I'm married to my best friend. A guy that makes me laugh 'til I can't breathe and one who steals my breath every time he walks into a room. I believe in happily ever after like the rising of the sun depended on it.

If you'd like to find out more about my books, visit my website. http://yvettehines.com

Made in the USA
Lexington, KY
17 July 2013